Princess Juniper
OF TORR

Princess Juniper

OF TORR

AMMI-JOAN PAQUETTE

PHILOMEL BOOKS

Also by Ammi-Joan Paquette:

Princess Juniper of the Hourglass

Princess Juniper of the Anju

PHILOMEL BOOKS
an imprint of Penguin Random House LLC
375 Hudson Street, New York, NY 10014

Copyright © 2017 by Ammi-Joan Paquette.
Lower Continent map © 2015 by Dave Stevenson.
Torr Castle map © 2017 by Dave Stevenson.
Penguin supports copyright. Copyright fuels creativity, encourages diverse voices, promotes free speech, and creates a vibrant culture. Thank you for buying an authorized edition of this book and for complying with copyright laws by not reproducing, scanning, or distributing any part of it in any form without permission. You are supporting writers and allowing Penguin to continue to publish books for every reader.

Philomel Books is a registered trademark of Penguin Random House LLC.

Library of Congress Cataloging-in-Publication Data
Names: Paquette, Ammi-Joan, author.
Title: Princess Juniper of Torr / Ammi-Joan Paquette.
Description: New York, NY : Philomel Books, [2017]. | Series: Princess Juniper ; 3
Summary: "Princess Juniper must rescue her father and kingdom from outside invaders"—
Provided by publisher. | Identifiers: LCCN 2016030433 | ISBN 9780399171536 (hardback)
Subjects: | CYAC: Princesses—Fiction. | Kings, queens, rulers, etc.—Fiction. | Adventure and adventurers—Fiction. | BISAC: JUVENILE FICTION / Royalty. | JUVENILE FICTION / Action & Adventure / General. | JUVENILE FICTION / Social Issues / Friendship.
Classification: LCC PZ7.P2119 Pt 2017 | DDC [Fic]—dc23
LC record available at https://lccn.loc.gov/2016030433

Printed in the United States of America.
ISBN 9780399171536
1 3 5 7 9 10 8 6 4 2
Edited by Jill Santopolo.   Design by Siobhán Gallagher.   Text set in 12.5 pt. Perpetua.

For Jill Santopolo:
for making all of this possible

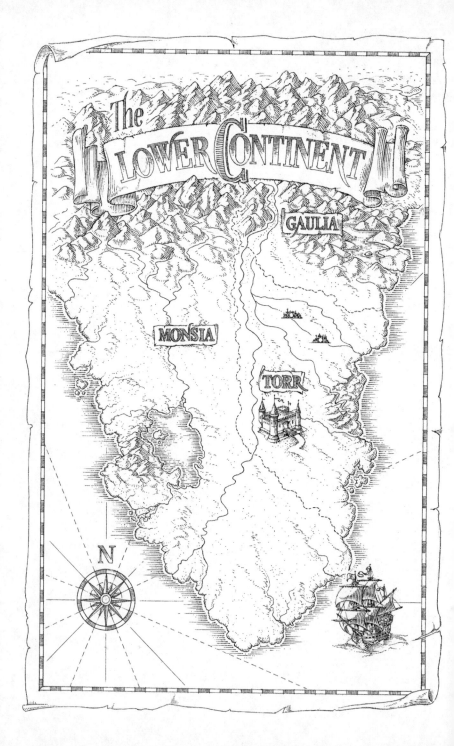

The Game Plan and the Players
Core Team

Princess Juniper Torrence: Ruler of Queen's Basin, excessive planner, sometimes-worrier, unafraid of a hard day's work (new life skill!).

Erick Dufrayne: Queen's chief adviser, incurable bookworm, deep thinker, knows a little bit of everything there is to know (and can find the rest in his volumes).

Alta Mavenham: Head guard of Queen's Basin, supremely skilled soldier, fearless, loyal to the core.

Tippy Larson: Queen's maid, life of every party, eager young prankster, frolicking and playful always.

Wildcards

Cyril Lefarge: Son of King Regis's traitorous chief adviser, former bully who is lately turning into a pretty decent fellow.

Jessamyn (Jess) Ceward: Recast from an uppity layabout into an energetic young spymaster—a skill she learned from her father, Rogett Ceward, spy-for-hire (now imprisoned in the castle).

Root Bartley: Cyril's best friend and former henchman, now solidly loyal to Queen's Basin; boy-of-all-trades and invaluable helper.

Oona Dell: Middle Dell sibling, who made some poor choices in the past but recently settled down and became part of the team again.

Support Staff

Paul Perigor: Master of all green and growing things; soulful character; creative in all ways.

Leena Ogilvy: A true lady-of-the-foods; runs the kitchen with energy and flair; pretty much the most important person around, all things considered.

Roddy Rodin: Master woodworker and craftsman; if you pair his crafting skill with Erick's creative mind for inventions, what can they not do?

Toby Dell: The eldest of the Dell siblings; has a magic touch with the animals and has taken charge of their care.

Sussi Dell: Youngest of the Dells; easygoing and friendly in nature; doer of all that needs doing.

Filbert Terrafirm: The much-needed brawn of the group; lends his strength and bulk wherever it's needed.

External Contacts

Zetta of the Anju: Newly minted ruler of the Anju tribe; my recent rival; a fearless and honorable girl I am proud to call my friend.

Mother Odessa: An elder of the Anju and my long-lost grandmother; spending more time getting to know her is something I plan to do as soon as possible.

Eglantine Ceward: Our mystery contact within the palace; elder sister of Jessamyn; ignored by the invaders due to her youth and deafness; our key ally in the plan to retake Torr Castle.

Things I Have Learned as the Ruler of Queen's Basin
by Princess Juniper Torrence

#1: It pays to dream big!

It was little more than a month ago that I set out to build a country of my very own, high in the Hourglass Mountains: just me and my thirteen subjects. Now our tiny kingdom of Queen's Basin is thriving and we are ready to take on our next challenge.

#2: Being queen is harder than it looks.

Maybe *thriving* isn't the best word. We have had some huge setbacks, including a challenge to my throne (which I neatly took care of) and most recently a devastating flood that destroyed much of the work we'd done in building up our settlement.

#3: True friends are worth their weight in berries.

Despite the difficulties, Queen's Basin is now stronger than ever, and that is all thanks to its wonderful citizens. We've grown ever so close—instead of the obstacles pulling us apart, each one we've faced has only made us a tighter group. Every person here has become a true friend!

#4: Worry never disappears, but keeping busy helps.

My biggest worry, every single day, is for the fate of my father and the kingdom of Torr. The night our group left for the Hourglass Mountains, Torr Castle was invaded. My father was captured and put in prison, along with the whole of his guard and all the loyal castle subjects. My father ordered our group to stay hidden up here, and we have done so until now. But that is about to change.

#5: Planning and list making are extremely valuable assets.

Torr has been invaded by the Monsian army. We are a group of fourteen kids. We are small, but we are mighty. I . . . do not have a complete plan yet. But figuring one out is the very next thing on my schedule.

#6: It's never too late to learn something new.

The newest thing in my life has been getting to know the Anju, my mother's people, who live the next mountain over from us. After some adventures, we have forged a sort of alliance with them. I suspect they will be quite essential as we move to reclaim Torr.

#7: People really can change, sometimes in the most surprising ways.

A great surprise of the last few weeks has been the transformation of my cousin Cyril. A lifelong bully of my childhood, he was caught up in his father's plot to betray King Regis and aid the Monsian invasion. Recently he has shown an entirely new side, however, and he and I have found common ground at long last.

#8: Fiery dracos are real. (I know, right?!)

Zetta, the newly appointed teenage leader of the Anju, has managed to befriend an enormous fire salamander—better known as the fire-breathing draco of legend. She's called him Floris, and he's quite tame to her, but let any others cross him at their peril!

#9: There's not much that a good dance party can't cure.

Finally: I started Queen's Basin because I wanted a place where every person could find their own glow, could be who they truly wanted to be. I am a princess, and a queen, but I'm also a girl. And sometimes there's nothing that fits the moment better than putting on your dancing slippers, cranking up the old Musicker, and pumping out some tunes till the moon goes dark. Our next big party, I hope, will be held in the safety of the reclaimed walls of Torr Castle.

1

LEAVING QUEEN'S BASIN WAS PROVING HARDER
than Juniper had expected.

She'd spent a little over a month as queen of her very own tiny
mountain country, ruling over the best group of young subjects
around. Even the superheated flash flood that had swept through
just days ago had not beaten them. Their settlement wasn't yet
rebuilt—that would take time, which they didn't have right now—
but though a little scruffier and more pockmarked than before, it
was still their bowl-shaped, sun-dappled valley home.

It was still Queen's Basin.

Now, though, it was time to turn their minds to bigger things:
Time to face the enemy head-on. Time to save King Regis. Time to
head back to Torr.

Their saddlebags were stuffed with the last of their food supplies, and the horses they'd gotten back from the Anju were rested
and raring to go. Two days ago, an early scouting team of Alta and
Jess had ventured down the mountain to see what they could learn

about the state of Torr. The scouts were due back any time now; if all went as planned, the whole group would head out tomorrow morning.

Around Juniper, the valley was quiet in the dim evening light. But she could hear a buzz of activity coming from just up the mountain. With a grin, Juniper scrambled along the cliffside path. She pushed through the hanging bluevines into the Great Cave. There they all were: her fellow citizens of Queen's Basin. Her friends. Nearly a dozen kids were jumbled in the giant cave room, each one bright-eyed and yammering as they went about their tasks: packing and repacking, triple-checking, all desperately busy on this last night before the big departure.

"Princess Juniper!" called a deep voice to her left. It was Root, looking anxious. "Have you seen Cyril?"

"Cyril?" Juniper frowned. Since their return from the Anju adventure, her cousin had reformed his bullying ways and had stopped spying for his traitorous father and the invading Monsians. He'd joined the group for meals and done chores alongside the others. But when *was* the last time she'd seen him? "Not since breakfast," she said slowly.

"Nor I," said Root. "He said he wanted some time alone—I didn't think anything of it. But now . . ."

Juniper felt her stomach clench. Root was Cyril's best friend. If *he* didn't know where Cyril was, what did that mean?

"Come on," she said. "Let's figure this out."

Against the far wall, Erick stood under a flaming wall sconce, completely absorbed by a clothbound volume entitled *Treatise of the*

Stone: Lower Continental Maneuvers and Outmaneuvers over the Centuries.

"We might have a problem," Juniper called out. Looking up and seeing them, Erick whipped the book behind his back, clearly ashamed to be caught reading at such a busy time. Actually, though, anything else from him would have been weird. Nearby, Leena stopped brushing her horse and moved in closer to see what was going on.

"Have either of you seen Cyril since breakfast?" Juniper asked them.

Erick and Leena exchanged a look. Both shook their heads.

"Could he have gone climbing and met some accident?" asked Erick.

"Not likely," said Root. He cleared his throat. "The thing is, his horse isn't where it ought to be. He keeps it tethered right next to mine. His saddlebags are gone, too."

"You think he's left us?" Erick said incredulously.

"Why, that leech-faced lout!" Leena exclaimed. "I *knew* his goodsy turnabout was too neat to be true! Once a traitor, always a traitor, that's what I say."

"Hold up, now," Juniper said. "Let's not jump to conclusions. Cyril's made some bad choices in the past, but that doesn't mean he's not changed. There might still be a reasonable explanation for this. He could have gone . . ."

There was an awkward silence. Juniper met Erick's eye. Where *could* Cyril have gone, with his horse and loaded saddlebags, and the group's departure just around the corner? And with no word to anyone of what he had in mind?

"There's nowhere he could be that he *ought* to be," said Erick quietly. "We move out as a group—that was always the plan. We all agreed."

Juniper thought of Cyril as he was weeks ago: hectoring, challenging, conniving. She thought of their recent exchanges, how he'd grown to be almost more of a brother than a cousin.

There must be some explanation. There *must*.

"We just hammered out our starting plan last night, didn't we?" said Leena. "Set up the details for how and when we'd get in to the castle: legging it with the crowds until Summerfest, then sneaking inside the walls during the open celebration. Well? No sooner did he hear the news but that boy saw his chance and skedaddled."

"No," said Juniper.

Seeing their next steps all set out in the open, had Cyril reconsidered what he owed his father, the traitorous Monsian ally Lefarge? Or, worse, had Cyril been lying to them, to *her*, all along?

Had Cyril ever truly been on their side?

"I don't like to doubt him," said Erick. "Maybe there's another explanation."

Leena snorted, and even Root looked pained. Juniper didn't like it, either. Over the last few weeks, across the Anju Trials and all the difficulties there, Juniper had grown closer to Cyril than she'd ever thought possible. She'd seen a different side of her cousin than he had shown during their childhood. It seemed impossible to imagine him out there now, spilling their plans to the Monsians, bulking up the defenses around the captive king, and preparing Torr Castle against their incursion. Yet what else could explain him sneaking away without a word to anyone?

The more they discussed and looked at all the angles, the clearer the plain facts stood out. Cyril was gone, along with his horse and his travel gear and up-to-date knowledge of how they planned to get inside Torr Castle.

Oh, the cut went deep! Juniper clenched her fists and stared at the wall, while the others muttered around her.

She'd been a fool to trust him. She saw that now. They just had to face the facts.

Cyril had betrayed them again.

WITH EFFORT, JUNIPER PULLED HERSELF together. She squeezed her churning emotions into a hard ball and flung them to the back of her mind. From now on, she wouldn't spare that blackguard one further thought.

Next to her, Erick was watching with a half grin.

"What?" Juniper said, startled out of her funk. "What's that gleam in your eye?"

Leena, too, cracked a smile. "Only you're that predictable, Princess Juniper," she said.

Erick nodded. "It's like a whole three-act play just unfolded across your face. We're now at the stage where our intrepid hero has settled upon a firm course of action and dives into it with verve and vigor."

Despite herself, Juniper laughed. "I wouldn't say my course is at all firm right now. But I'm hanged if I'm going to let Cyril botch up everything we've been working for. Let's get the rest of the team together, shall we? An emergency meeting is in order."

"Calling a meeting without your indispensable scouting party?" came a voice behind them. "I see we've made it back just in time."

"Why, 'tis our own Alta, alive and in the flesh!" Tippy's shrill voice trumpeted up from suspiciously nearby. Apparently she'd been lurking in their conversation. Now, though, her voice was loud enough to bring over the rest of the group as she bounded toward the new arrivals.

Alta was leading her magnificent stallion, Thunderstar, with Jess and the fine-boned Lady clattering close behind. The girls' eyes were bright and their cheeks flushed from the long tramp through the cave tunnels. With a squeal, Tippy launched herself at Alta, who reached down to enfold the younger girl in a full-body embrace.

"Well met," Juniper said to the scouts, once the hugfest was done. "Your timing could not be better."

"We're all packed up for tomorrow's out-leaving, only just awaiting your return, and also we've had Cyril gad off us, so he's a traitor all over again," Tippy summarized, all in a rush.

This was met with alarm from the larger group. Juniper waved her arms in the air. "All right, then, the news is out: It seems Cyril's gone and left us without a word. We don't know his reasons, but I think it's safe to assume the worst." Juniper sighed. "Still, we're set to head out tomorrow at dawn, and there's no way to push that any sooner. The scouts and their mounts need a night's rest, and we can catch up on their news meanwhile. Plus, we've some powerful planning to do. Which, as with anything, is better done with food near at hand. Shall we regroup at the dining area?"

The others agreed and quickly went about finishing the last of their packing before heading from the cave. Alta began tethering Thunderstar, but Jess went straight for a low pouch hanging between Lady's hind legs. She reached inside and pulled out a warm, purring bundle.

Tippy perked up immediately. "Fleeter! Ah, my own Fleeter is back, too! May I hold your little spy cat, Jess? I've missed him so."

Jess rolled her eyes, but still seemed to appreciate Tippy's enthusiasm. Certainly they were the only two who saw any appeal in the mangy creature (which legitimately looked part moth-eaten sweater and part undead corpse). Oblivious to Juniper's faint shudder, Tippy and Fleeter got busy nuzzling, so she left well enough alone and headed down into the Basin.

Within a few minutes, all the Queen's Basin crew had trundled down the winding cliffside path and settled themselves on the worn sitting stones. The torches had been brought from the cave and set up around their dining area, where the flames scratched long shadows on the ring of anxious faces. Leena passed around a basket of day-old biscuits along with Root's latest efforts at dried meat—quail and summer hare—which was extraordinarily tough, but filling. The effort of chewing also offered some distraction from the worries at hand.

"The meat needs more salt, I think," tried Root. He was looking around as though trying to gauge the success of his curing skills.

"Fleeter loves it," Tippy declared.

"Makes us work for every bite, is all," said Roddy, and a few others murmured agreement.

8

"I think it's quite perfect just as it is," said Oona. Her hand lifted as though she was going to put it on Root's knee (she was sitting so close to him that she barely had to move to do so), but at the last minute, she seemed to think better of it. She blushed and lowered her eyes.

"So," Juniper said, turning to Alta, "what news do you have to share of your scouting mission?"

"The journey went—" Alta began.

"Quite as well as expected," Jess cut in. Alta scowled at the interruption, but Jess barreled on. "We visited Sari first, as it's the nearest town to us and on our way. We passed quickly through, for as usual they have no concerns but for their own industry and care not a fig for the goings-on of the greater country."

Being the daughter of a renowned spy-for-hire seemed to have given Jess the right flair for this scouting mission, Juniper thought. "So you didn't stay over there?" she asked.

"Only an afternoon," Alta confirmed. "Then we made our way to Longton, arriving by nightfall."

Jess nodded. "Longton was its usual hotbed of useful information."

"How did you go about collecting it?" Leena asked.

"In my experience, the best information is gathered by spending time in public places—parks and festivals, marketplaces, alehouses."

"Surely not an alehouse!" exclaimed Sussi.

"Well, they didn't allow us in, being young and unaccompanied and all," Jess conceded. "But then we found a spot even better: an open-air theater putting on a play of *Belle and the Moon*."

"Belle and the Moon?" Juniper whispered. The others didn't know it, but this play—and its title song—had a very special meaning to her. It was not only her favorite musical performance, but also the last song she had danced to with her father, on that night that seemed so long ago, her thirteenth Nameday celebration back at the palace. Before any of this had happened—before Queen's Basin, before their departure.

Before the Monsians had invaded and taken her father captive.

It was all too easy to get caught up in the day-to-day stress and drama and tasks that needed doing, and to forget the harsh reality that was hanging over them. They were no longer out here to play and have a good time in their carefree summer kingdom. They truly had to be—or had to *become* at least—a compact fighting force, a miniature all-kids army that the enemy would not see coming.

Somehow, some way, they had to save the day.

Oblivious to Juniper's inner turmoil, Jess was still recounting the news they had gathered on their scouting expedition. "Word from across Torr is slim and grim. The Monsians did march down the White Highway some weeks back, but they made no stops other than to set some fields ablaze. And that seemed more to make a point than anything."

"Them's the fires we saw from here! Clouds of fearsome smoke everywhere!" Tippy shuddered and clutched Fleeter more tightly.

Jess nodded. "The Monsians brought their might against the palace, and were through the walls in a matter of days. It was an inside job, folks say, that's how they got in so quick. Betrayed from within."

None of this was news, of course. The betrayal of Rupert Lefarge, the king's chief adviser and Cyril's father, was the reason Torr Castle had fallen. But, oh, that did not make it any easier to hear. Those walls had stood for centuries! Down through countless generations of Torrence rulers, not once had the defenses been breached. Juniper clenched her hands into fists.

"Several armed battalions remain at the castle," said Alta, "perhaps one or two hundred soldiers."

Erick frowned, and Juniper could guess why. His father had been captain of the guard at the palace. If the Monsian soldiers were loose in the castle, what must be the state of the Torrean guards?

Alta went on, "Now, here's a curious thing. Apparently the palace is not being ruled by the Monsians, but by Rupert Lefarge and his wife, Malvinia. They've been putting out the word that everything across the country should carry on as normal. Including, and especially, Summerfest."

Jess nodded. "They've been sending out a great tide of pamphlets and proclamations, urging townsfolk and villagers to attend. Talking it up as an extraordinary spectacle like nothing that's come before it. And there is to be a particular announcement on the final day that no one will want to miss."

"It's good they're not changing the Summerfest plans," said Juniper. Their own palace entry relied on that festival, after all.

But she didn't like the sound of the rest of it. Not one single bit.

"And no one suspected your origins as you gathered your intelligence?" Leena asked.

Jess raised both eyebrows, as if the question was beneath her. She walked over to Tippy and picked up the sleeping Fleeter, settling the cat in the folds of her skirt. Then she pulled a small jar from her pocket and began dabbing her face with cream.

Alta said, "We stayed the night in Longton—this antiquated costume shop owner we sat next to at the show was selling off his stock and taking in boarders, saving up to pursue his lifelong dream of becoming a squid trawler." Juniper blinked at this information, and Alta shrugged. "It gave us a base for launching our investigations, with no one the wiser."

"So there's the news," said Juniper. The meal had wound down, and Root was passing around a bowlful of hazelnuts. Doggone things—where *did* he keep getting them? Now with bellies satisfied and this new information heavy on their minds, the settlers were getting restless.

"We *had* ourselves a sound plan," Leena said, her voice sharp, "before Cyril ran amok on us. What do we do now?"

"Yes," said Oona. "How does all this change things for us?"

Jess screwed the lid back on her jar and waited with the rest.

Juniper climbed to her feet. The truth was, she had no idea. But what she did know was their starting point. And as any good list maker knows, once you scratch that *#1* on the page, you're as good as halfway to your goal. "All right. Listen up, Queen's Basin," she said. "Let's recap what we know. Starting with Summerfest."

"Summerfest!" trumpeted Tippy, popping up to bob around Juniper like a gourd-doll set to rocking. "Only the most glorious time of the year! Seven days of food and frolic in the summer sun."

"Kicks off in just over a week," said Leena. "Back in my palace days, we were sweating in the kitchen for ages leading up to it, getting everything ready for the crowds."

Juniper nodded. "It has always been my father's favorite festival," she said quietly. "It's a tradition that goes back to his father's father, who wanted a time when the citizens of Torr—so many as cared to join in—could mingle and refresh themselves all together in one place." Juniper had so many memories of Summerfest in years past: watching the slippery butterfight wrestlers duke it out for the crowds, the taste of sticky spun-sugar confections on her tongue, the tangled riot of noise and crowds that gave off a gauzy freedom she felt at no other time. Summerfest had always been one of the highlights of her year. But this year, things could not have been more different.

Thousands of townspeople and villagers from all across Torr traveled every summer to the castle for the chance to attend— or even to be on the outskirts, for not all of the gathered thousands could make it into the castle proper. In the weeks building up to the end of summer, tent cities were erected in the fields outside the castle grounds. Closer to the gates, the shopkeepers, tradesmen, and performers set up their stalls. These next few weeks would be packed with people and buzzing with activity. And this year, it looked like there might be even more attending than usual.

In short? There was no better place for a small rebel group to hide in plain sight.

"So the grand palace opening on Summerfest Eve has been the linchpin of our plan thus far," said Juniper. The Queen's Basin group had planned to lurk among the festivalgoers during the week leading up to the festival, using the cover of the crowd to gain information on the Monsian presence in the palace: enemy plans, placement, fortifications. They would then make their move during the grand feast that was traditionally held the evening before Summerfest. In all the hullabaloo of partying crowds, no one would notice a stealthy stream of kids joining the greater throngs to gain access to the palace. Once inside, the kids would go right to work freeing the king and reclaiming the castle.

The details of said rescue, admittedly, had yet to be worked out. That first step was solid, though.

Or at least, it *had* been.

Juniper sighed. "But now we need to rethink everything. Cyril knows our plan. He'll be expecting us. So let's think about it: What will *his* first step be upon leaving here?"

"Make a beeline back to the palace," said Erick. "Spill our info. Then have all the guards lined up and ready. On Summerfest Eve, they're alert and on the lookout. They spot us; they pounce."

"Even more than that," said Alta, "I bet he'll send guards into the festival grounds well before the fest begins. He'll be looking for you and us all so he can foil our plans before they start."

"He won't even let us set foot in the castle," said Sussi, her voice quivering.

"We should count on more security around King Regis, too," said Jess, "now they know someone's set to try a rescue. And we should probably prepare for the worst: The king wasn't to be moved until after the festival? If I were the bad guys, I would try to get him out sooner. Pack him right off on his way *before* it even starts. Stop any chance of subterfuge cold."

Juniper felt the familiar tightening inside her chest. *Don't lose focus,* she told herself. But how on earth could they best an occupying army? They were just thirteen kids, after all. Zetta of the Anju had promised help if it came down to a fight, but she wouldn't march her people in blindly without knowing what was going on. No, their only weapons had been secrecy and the element of surprise.

And now what were they left with?

Juniper looked around her at the ring of dispirited faces. This had been hard enough when they *did* have a solid plan. Now the group felt perilously close to falling apart.

Still unsure what to do, Juniper cleared her throat. The chatter died away.

"Oh, boy," said Tippy in a dramatic whisper. "It's time for a speech, innit?"

Juniper smiled weakly. "You know me well, Tipster!" She cleared her throat again, sharpening her focus. *All right,* actually she was stalling for time. Finally she said, "I'm not going to lie to you: This is a low blow we've been dealt. Cyril's duplicity has us right back at the starting gate. But we've been well pummeled before. And have we let that stop us?" A mutter went around the circle.

"We've faced storm and flood, we've built a country all our own, we've lived alone in the wild, and we've *thrived*. We are overcomers. We are the children of Torr! And now? Without a doubt, we are Torr's only hope. So." She paused. Something was niggling at her from earlier in the conversation.

And with it, the spark of an idea.

Juniper turned to Alta and Jess. "I've been thinking about that place you stayed in Longton," she said.

Jess made a hawking sound in her throat. "That renegade silk-stitcher."

Juniper beamed. "Ah, yes. About the silk. And cotton and velvet and leather and lace! That's *exactly* what caught my attention. Now listen up, for I have a new plan that might help us not only outsmart Cyril but get the jump on our whole enemy besides. First, we'll need to break into two groups."

"Huh?" Tippy's eyes were round as an owl's.

"Yep," said Juniper. "One group will head straight for the castle. And the other? Will do a little dressing up."

Team Goshawk

Members: Juniper—Erick—Jess—Leena—Root—
Oona—Tippy

Motto: Blaze the trail . . . trail the blaze.

Mission: Infiltrate, investigate, initiate.

Team Bobcat

Members: Alta—Paul—Toby—Sussi—Roddy—Filbert

Motto: The best guise is a *dis*guise.

Mission: Hide in plain sight; be ready for anything.

3

"PSSST!" CAME A VOICE IN THE DARK.

Juniper startled awake, nearly hitting her head on the low roof of her bedchamber in the hollowed-out heart of the Great Tree's trunk. Pulling her covers around her against the night chill, she squirmed out onto the landing. There on the tree house's wood-plank floor stood Jess, looking perfectly put together in tight curls and crisp riding dress. The pale morning light—*was* it even morning yet?—filtering through the tree's leafy canopy set Jess's teeth glinting and her powdered cheeks shining.

"What are you doing here?" Juniper whispered, not wanting to wake Tippy, who was sleep-mumbling in the bedroom nook above Juniper's. "It's nowhere near time to set out yet."

"I've been thinking a little more about this plan," said Jess, "and our dastardly Cyril, and your very well-known appearance."

"My very what—?"

"Princess Juniper," said Jess, "from the time I was knee-high to a ferret, I've seen your face everywhere I looked: paintings, dioramas, performances. You've got the best-known mug in the Lower Continent, I reckon."

Juniper scoffed, but Jess smirked at her. "No need to deny it. But don't you worry a wink. I've got a special party trick, and I'm all ready to share." She raised one hand to show a small corked bottle and a sharp pair of scissors.

Haircutting scissors.

A full hour later, Juniper peered sidewise at the rippling surface of the Lore River as they walked alongside it. Their looking glass had been lost in the flood, so it was hard to clearly see the changes that Jess's scissors and dark mystery bottle had worked. Juniper jiggled her sleeve so that the bone-handled comb she kept there slid out. She ran the comb through her newly short locks.

"Do I look very different?" she asked.

Jess shrugged. "Not your face, of course. And not to anyone who knows you well. But the outer trappings are brand-new." One side of her mouth edged up in an approving smile.

Juniper squinted again at the water's surface. Truthfully, she felt worlds different. Jess had hacked off her long russet curls to chin-length, and had doused what remained in a black walnut tincture that left them a rich, nutty brown. Her disguise was finished by exchanging her beloved blue traveling gown for a well-tailored pair of trousers and a thick woolen vest and surcoat. She did insist on keeping the snow-white cloak that had belonged to her mother, lately given her by Mother Odessa. Jess had grudgingly agreed;

after all, Juniper had gotten the cloak after leaving the palace, so it would not be recognizable.

"Aghast!" Tippy bleated as she whirled up to them, then fell dramatically to her knees. "Why, Your Most Pitifully Shorn Majesty, what has that weevily girl done to you? To your hair and your—your—gown and—"

Alta stepped up and studied Juniper, then grinned. "I know you were sick of that fancy braided updo after Cyril's takedown party, but I didn't realize things were *this* bad."

The others were gathering now, too, pulled in by Tippy's loud bluster, which showed no signs of stopping.

"The locks of deepest auburn, all gone . . ." Tippy wailed.

"Hush now," Juniper said finally. "I'm not so very different as all that!"

"I daresay you could pass all but the closest inspection," Jess said proudly. "Cyril and the guards are bound to be scanning from a distance. They'll have no time to study each face up close, so long as we stay out of their way."

"Good thinking," said Erick. "I like it."

The others agreed, with the exception of Tippy, who stayed stubbornly bereft. But what was done was done, and even she finally conceded defeat. The group moved up to the Great Cave as the sun rose over the Basin.

It was nearly time for their adventure to begin.

At the cave's entrance, Juniper turned for one last look at their rough little country: the stone walkways they had painstakingly wedged back into place after the flood; the dining area with its stout ring of sitting-stone boulders that had not given an inch to the waters; the warm and welcoming Great Tree, with its secret branch-stairs and the hidden chambers at its heart. These places had become so much a part of her over these past summer weeks. She couldn't believe she was really leaving.

No. Not *leaving*. Not really, not for good.

It was only stepping away for a moment, to make them all safe in preparation for the group's eventual return.

On the North Bank, the wildflowers still glowed in a deep blue carpet. If such beauty could come out of total destruction—blooming as they had, overnight, after the flash flood that had torn the valley apart—then how much more could she, too, surmount the obstacles and go on?

Queen's Basin would always be in Juniper's heart. And she'd be back—they all would—and *soon*. She would make sure of it.

But now Torr was calling them.

Within the hour, the two teams—headed by Juniper (Goshawk) and Alta (Bobcat)—were saddled up and ready to go. They would each head out separately, since two smaller bands of kids would be less noticeable than one big one.

Team Goshawk would take the lead, as they had to travel all the way to the castle, and a hard ride it would be to make it by day's end. Their first trek to the Basin had taken them much longer. But of course they'd had slow-moving carts and carriages with them then. Today they were fleet of foot and boundless of energy.

Today they had a mission.

"Not even my long hair to weigh me down," declared Juniper, flouncing her new bob. She found that she quite liked the tickle of air on the back of her neck, how light her head felt without its bulky tresses. It was like putting down a burden she hadn't known she was carrying, shucking off her royal mantle for a bit and being someone entirely new.

She seemed to be doing that quite a lot these days, come to think of it: finding new shades of herself that she hadn't known existed. What else might be lying in store, she wondered, just waiting to be uncovered?

With a shiver of anticipation, she nudged her well-packed mount across the rocky floor of the Great Cave to where Alta stood tightening the strap on her last saddlebag. "Six days from today, don't forget," Juniper told her. "We'll come and find you."

Alta nodded. "By that time, we'll be well meshed in with the teeming gaggle of Summerfesters, you have my word."

From here, Goshawk would go straight into the castle: no delays, no waiting. Last night, they had launched the messenger (the king's highly trained ghost bat, their letter carrier), asking Jess's sister Eglantine to leave the back cellar door unlocked: This would be their way into the palace. Once inside, they would sneak and lurk about, gathering what information they could. Team Bobcat would wait an hour after Goshawk first left, putting distance between the two groups. Then Bobcat would set out for Longton on the first step of their own mission: procure costumes. They would make their way down to the castle grounds, joining the Summerfest throngs and able to move about in plain sight without suspicion. The two groups would then reunite and use the intelligence gathered to plan the final assault.

As plans went, it was rough as nettlekin. But it was a start. A plan in motion was a plan they could work with; it was just a matter of piecing together the puzzle as they went for the best fit.

"Journey well, then," said Juniper, with a lump in her throat. The members of Team Bobcat stood by their horses, identical looks of anxious excitement on their faces.

"Good-bye, Alta, my summer big sister!" Tippy sobbed from her mount, a moist handkerchief in her hand. "Good-bye, all of you Bobcats. And good-bye most of all to our own QB. Who knows when ever we shall return?"

"Queen's Basin isn't going anywhere," said Juniper. "And we may be back here sooner than we think. I know I plan to return just as soon as I'm able—and how could I travel anywhere without my lady's maid on-the-go?"

Tippy hiccupped and nodded, then looked up with a smile on her tearstained face. "I just had to get all that out of me, Your Very Short-Haired Juniper. I reckon I feel good to go on now. QB will stay with me right here." She thumped her chest.

"Me too, Tippy," whispered Juniper. "Me too."

Finally, all was done that needed doing and all was said that needed saying. Juniper and the rest of Team Goshawk waved good-bye to their friends, then they turned and set off down the cave corridor.

The next adventure had begun.

4

"IS IT TIME FOR EATS YET?" ASKED OONA, SOME hours later. They'd navigated the caves with little trouble and were now bushwhacking through the dense forest, heading toward the White Highway, which led south to the castle.

"It can't be long till we reach the main road," said Leena. "We've been slogging these trails for the nighthawk's hours!"

They *had* been pushing hard, but their plan hinged on getting right inside the castle grounds. To have any chance at *that*, they had to arrive under cover of darkness—and while Eglantine's door remained unlocked.

"We shan't want to stop for a proper meal," Juniper called to Oona. "We've got ever so much ground to cover to make the castle by nightfall. Let's try and eat as we go. You've got your provisions sack, right? We'll stop to stretch our legs once we get farther along, if there's time."

Oona frowned. As Juniper clicked to bring up her pace, she

noticed Root sidling his mount near Oona and handing her a little woven bag, which the girl received with a soppy smile.

"I still question the safety of our gamboling so brazenly along the great highway," Jess called from behind. Her words rang over the muffled hoofbeats in the forest glade. "Are there no back roads we might take? Surely that would reduce our visibility at little cost to speed."

Juniper shook her head. "You and Alta both said the highway was packed with travelers, and should be still more so now, another day closer to Summerfest."

"Packed is a good thing?" Leena asked from Juniper's other side.

"It is indeed. Think about it: Every able-bodied Torrean is heading for the palace right now—or will be soon—in order to be there for Summerfest. What better cover could we have than to lose ourselves in the unwashed throngs? We won't stand out one bit, for who would notice a rough thread in a rougher rug?"

"Ruffians we have aplenty," said Erick, from up ahead. He was riding Gentle Giant, a huge silver thoroughbred who pretty much guided himself. That was a good thing, as it left Erick free to do what he did best: read. He was leafing steadily through the map book splayed across his lap, looking up just in time to swat a sweet-gum branch out of the way before it lashed him across the face. Soon, just Gentle Giant's swishing tail could be seen, disappearing into a patch of bright daylight.

Juniper picked up her pace to join him, with the others close on her heels.

Without bulky wheels to slow them down, they'd cut clear through the dense forest, coming out at a different spot from where they'd gone in. Rather than riding the rutted Monsian Highway—a shivery proposition at any time, and the more so during this time of invasion—they now emerged at the very mouth of the White Highway. This great wide way would take them right down to Torrence town.

The Highway stretched below them, jammed and bustling with travelers: richly dressed nobles riding fine mounts; brightly painted carts advertising all sorts of wares; wagons packed with large families, round-bellied pups running along behind. All were part of the teeming masses making their way toward Summerfest.

"Well." Jess sniffed loudly. "The rabble certainly has grown since this time yesterday. I daresay your plan of blending in should work."

"Won't it, though?" Juniper said with a grin. "Even better than I'd expected. What say you, Tipster?"

Tippy squinted down at the bustling road, then back at Juniper. She grinned roguishly. "I say that your makeover wins the prize for top costume after all."

Leena and Erick laughed out loud, and even Jess allowed a smile.

"I shall take that as high praise from such an admirer of my Princess Juniper look as yourself," said Juniper gravely. "Shall we sally forth to the throngs, then?" She nudged her mare's flank—she was on the plump, spirited Sonsy—and girl and horse set off at a clatter down the rocky embankment toward the road. The other horses followed, single file.

Team Goshawk was soon absorbed into the roiling crowds making their way to Torr Castle.

After that, the journey got a lot more monotonous. The moving traffic separated itself into a fast column and a slow, but even the quick movers weren't nearly as peppy as Juniper would have liked. The packed crowds oozed along the road like treacle, until Juniper wanted to scream in frustration. To make things worse, she had to keep the hood of her white cloak pulled well over her face, for fear some sharp-eyed traveler might see through her disguise.

To pass the time as they plodded along, Juniper watched the scenery. Alta and Jess had reported no destruction in the cities of Sari and Longton, nor any Monsian presence whatsoever. Likewise there was no visible damage to the farmhouses, barns, or other buildings they passed on their way south. But the land was another story. What used to be thick, heavy fields of grain and corn, bursting with life and color, were now charred black wastelands.

"They set fire to the whole lot of them," Root muttered.

"I don't understand why anyone would do something like this," whimpered Oona.

"I'm not sure that violence needs a point," Juniper replied. "Sometimes it's just muscle flexing. A reminder to the weaker party of who's in charge." It was scary to think there was that kind of evil out there. And not only that, but *this* was the force they were trying to take down! Did their motley crew of kids really think they could liberate an entire country?

But no sooner had that thought buzzed into her head than Juniper squashed it flat. She was ruler of Queen's Basin, crown princess of Torr, and fierce girl on horseback. And this was the motley crew that *was* going to save King Regis and restore him to the throne of Torr if it was the last thing they did.

That was simply all there was to it.

Finally, *finally*, after the moon had risen overhead and the stars peered bright eyes down at them, the weary travelers crossed the Tricorn Bridge and approached the spires of Torr Castle. An unfamiliar banner snapped in the breeze, visible by the moon's dim light: the cur of Monsia. (It was actually a scarlet wolf, but Juniper refused to associate that barbaric nation with such a noble creature. They were dogs, nothing more.)

The crowds gradually thinned as the night wore on. With the festival still a week away, many of the travelers were stopping over in nearby cities, or resting at other points along the way. But others were already setting up camp in the giant field north of the castle—informally known as the Bazaar, though it lay empty most of the year—staking out land, setting up tents, erecting quick ramshackle buildings for their services or wares in the festivities to come. Despite the late hour, an energetic buzz filled the air. Torches and lanterns bobbed across the darkened field.

Moving steadily on from the late-night bustle of the Bazaar, the seven members of Team Goshawk were as quiet as the night around them. Even the clip-clop of the horses' hooves rang subdued on the packed ground.

"Let's hope that sister of yours delivers," said Leena with a yawn. "If she hasn't left that entryway unlocked, we'll be camping rough tonight."

"Egg always delivers," said Jess tightly. "If we can get inside the palace, she'll have done the rest. Count on it."

"This way," said Juniper. "The back supply route's rarely used, and the small gate it leads to is never guarded."

They took the deserted ring road around the castle, every step pulling them deeper into the hungry dark of night.

Ahead of them, the rusty jaws of Torr Castle loomed.

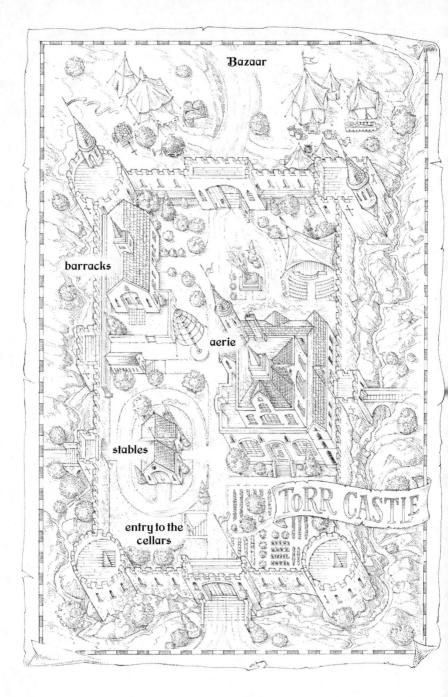

5

"I THOUGHT YOU SAID THE GATE WASN'T guarded!" Jess hissed in Juniper's ear.

It was only barest luck that had warned them in time—a barking cough, the creak of a hinge, a dull glint off the pommel of a sword—showing that the small gate up ahead was indeed under watch. To Juniper's eye, the guard seemed more than half asleep, but whatever his condition, just his being there barred their way in.

"New rulers bring new rules," said Juniper grimly. "I should have thought of that."

"Indeed," said Jess.

They'd pulled up behind a copse of trees around the bend from the gate. Based on the sentry's position, he hadn't noticed their approach, for the small relief that was. The first thing they'd done was dismount and secure their horses. Jess freed Fleeter from his nest and draped him around her neck like a cowl, then proceeded to stuff various items from her saddlebags into the pockets of her cloak. They had all packed light, but aside from a few small essentials, everything had to be left behind. (Hopefully they could come back for them eventually.) Now they needed a plan that would get them through this gate, and they needed it fast.

"Aren't there any other ways in?" asked Root.

"Not practically speaking," said Juniper. "Jess told Eglantine to unlock the door to the deep cellars, and this is the gate nearest that entry point. Going in elsewhere and tramping through acres of grounds will get us caught in no time."

"The other gates are surely even better guarded, in any case," said Erick. "It's hard to believe they even thought this one worth defending."

As gates went, it was a sorry specimen: barely bigger than a common doorway, the bars chewed with rust and swarmed by bluevines. In truth, Juniper had always had a soft spot for this gate, which was near the stables. On many a horse-riding lesson, she would canter past it just for the joy of looking and longing. It had always brought to mind a magical gateway to another world, a stepping-stone to mystery. Of course, before she'd always been on the inside, looking out.

How strange were the twisting turns of life!

"What we need," said Leena, yanking Juniper back into the moment, "is a distraction."

As they watched, the guard sighed heavily. He scuffed the ground with his boot, turned away from them, and sat down against the inside rail of the gate.

Juniper caught Root's eye. "I wonder. Do you suppose you might give this man a little midnight excitement?"

Root broke into a slow smile. "I reckon I could play the disoriented traveler."

"Excellent." It meant a change in plans for Root, as he'd be unable to follow them into the castle. But with his noble bearing, Juniper knew, he could well deflect any nosy questions and make his way to safety. "Lead him away from the gate as far as you can without looking suspicious. We'll make our move as soon as he's out of earshot."

"I believe I shall sing," said Root, and cleared his throat.

Oona's eyebrows had shot up in alarm at Juniper's words and now she moved closer to Root, but Leena yanked her arm. "He'll be fine."

"That I will," Root said, catching Oona's eye. Then to Juniper, "And I'll see to the horses as well, once you're safely through. I'll look for word from you however you're able to get it to me."

"Worst case, find the Bobcats—they should be joining the Bazaar before long."

Root nodded. "Now. Give me five minutes' head start, then get ready to dash." With that, he threw a leg over his mount and clicked low. His horse shot forward into the night.

The next few minutes passed in heart-wrenching flashes of action: Root cantering a wobbly path along the ring road toward the gate. Root swaying side to side in his saddle, launching into a loud, bawdy song that rang in all its tuneless glory up toward the dark sky. A grunt and a scuffle as the guard leaped to his feet. The earsplitting grind of a rusted gate, popping out on its hinges. Then the stampede of footsteps as the guard ran for a confrontation.

"Well done, Root!" said Juniper admiringly. She lifted a hand, and the six of them ghosted out from the trees and dashed toward the castle.

Down the road, Root raised the volume on his chantey. The guard was shouting now, and Juniper hoped Root wouldn't take the ruse too far and risk getting caught.

Flattening herself against the castle walls, she moved swiftly until she reached the bluevine-choked entryway. Coming up next to her, Tippy put a hand on the gate. "No!" said Juniper. "Don't move it a whisker—you heard that creak it made before? It'll bring our guard back in no time."

"I bet this gate hasn't been opened in years," said Jess, one hand cradled protectively around Fleeter, who still hung across her shoulders. "That guard did us a favor. We couldn't have gotten in without making a right racket."

As they moved through the gate, Juniper had to stop for a moment and blink away the film that gathered over her eyes. The gate was magical, after all.

It had led her home.

Based on the unexpected discovery of the guard at the gate, Juniper had no idea what other changes they might find inside the castle. A quick glance, though, showed no soldiers anywhere in sight. There were sure to be sentries on patrol or duty guards stationed up in the turrets; they would have to move carefully. But just this moment, inside the ancient stone walls of Torr Castle, the night was quiet as a cave.

A distant burst of laughter sounded outside, along with a man's gruff shout. But the sound carried more annoyance and frustration than anything else. The hoofbeats started up after a loud "Go on, then!" and Juniper knew Root was going to be all right.

"Now we're in," said Jess. "Let's go breach the palace."

They'd entered behind the stables, and they would need to circle the building entirely to reach their destination. Just inside those walls, Juniper knew, was her beloved mare, Butternut. *Soon,* she told herself. *One thing at a time.*

"Follow me," said Juniper in a low voice. "And let's keep as close to the walls as we can. We don't want to be out in the open where stray shadows might leap out and betray our presence."

"To who?" whispered Tippy.

"Anyone at all," said Leena decisively. "Better safe than baked in a pie, Cook always said."

Tippy's brow wrinkled in confusion. "That doesn't really make any—"

"Come *on*," said Jess. "Stuff your talk and keep up."

Across the grounds, nothing moved—not a flicker of wind nor a breath of air. Even the horses in the stable seemed to be sound asleep, to judge from the low hum coming from inside those walls. For her part, Juniper felt weirdly dreamlike. Was it really just a month since she'd said good-bye to these grounds, since she'd left with bulging carts and flowing hair and wild hopes for the future?

Since she'd last seen her father?

Her heartbeat quickened. Where were they keeping him?

Some part of her ached to run, to shout, to throw herself madcap at the enemy until they tossed him back out to her, safe and sound and unharmed.

Of course, life didn't work anything like that.

So she kept her hands flat against the mortared stones. She kept looking at each patch of ground before she set down her foot, checking for stray twigs or branches that might sound an alert.

But inside, she was ready. Oh, she was ready.

6

THEY MADE THEIR WAY LIKE THIS, PAST THE
stables and the exercise yard, to the edges of the back garden leading to the orchards. At this point, they left the wall behind and
cut through the trees, following the decorative marble-stone path.
Follow this trail to its end, Juniper knew, and they would reach the
soldiers' barracks—probably jammed now with snoring, snuffling
enemy troops. And plenty of wide-awake ones, like as not. Juniper
forced herself to go even slower, to make her steps more careful
and deliberate. They couldn't afford a single wrong move. In the
silence, every breath was a hurricane, the lightest footfall a shout.

They were moving in a loose pack now: Juniper leading the
way, Jess alongside her, and Erick, Leena, and Oona just behind.
And Tippy? Where had she gotten to?

Oh! There she was now, on the opposite side of the path, making a beeline for the narrow edging wall.

Tippy, who had never met a balancing surface she wouldn't
befriend.

Juniper dashed for Tippy. She couldn't call out, not without making a bigger ruckus. But it was too late. Tippy reached the ledge and leaped up in one nimble bound. She threw her hands out to each side, and paraded along it for a good ten steps before wind-milling her arms and toppling catastrophically off. The drop was less than knee-high, but that wasn't the problem. Juniper reached the wall just in time to land under Tippy. The two of them came down hard on the gravel path.

The crunch of clattering stones cracked the quiet like a gunshot.

There was a beat of silence. The six hung frozen in space.

Then, behind them, a horse in the stable whinnied. Loud. A little farther out, a hound barked.

Juniper shoved Tippy off her lap and leaped to her feet. "That's it for stealth," she said. "Let's get where we're going, and fast."

"Through here," said Leena, and ducked into the trees. "It's a smidge longer, but it gets us off the path."

They took off at a dead run: bushes grasping for them, branches clawing at their faces, innocent-looking flowers snapping hungrily at their ankles. When had the palace grounds gotten so *wild*? Finally they reached the end of the orchard and stood panting and peering out from the last row of trees at their destination. Just past the waist-high decorative hedge was a wide courtyard. From this, majestic as a whale cresting in the ocean, rose the palace.

It was the butt end of the palace, of course—the kitchens and workshops and sculleries and laundries. But the sight was no less beautiful to Juniper's eyes. Still, the very best thing about the view in front of them was this: darkness across every window, not a peep nor mutter from the building ahead of them. And below it, deep underground, were acres and acres of cellars.

Also known as? The way in.

"Let's play it safe," Juniper said. "We'll go one at a time: Clear the hedge, cross the yard, down the stairs. Everybody got it?"

The nods were tight, and Leena clung to Tippy's hand, making them an exception to the one-at-a-time rule. Jess led out first, darting so noiselessly in her dark cloak and silent shoulder-cat that Juniper couldn't help a smile of admiration. Jess's father was a fool not to see her value as a spy partner. The girl had clearly learned her desired trade well.

Their destination was a recessed hollow just beyond the back door to the darkened summer kitchen. Jess reached the spot and seemed to sink right into the ground. Erick followed next, then Oona, then Leena and Tippy. Juniper went last, looking first behind her to be sure they had not been spotted or followed.

The orchard was still as mirrored glass.

Juniper reached the recess panting slightly from her run—*she was no master spy, that was for sure!*—and joined the others at the bottom of the stone steps. The landing was sunk so low that their heads were below ground level. Excellent! The steps ended at a rough-looking wooden door, which Jess pushed open.

"Good Egg delivers," Jess whispered. "Told you so."

It crossed Juniper's mind that Jess sounded less pleased by this than Juniper would have expected. But then they slipped out of the dark night into the darker passageway, and all other thoughts fell away. Erick pushed the door shut and latched it behind them. Leena retrieved a torch and a striking stone from a wall sconce.

"Can we risk that light?" Jess asked.

"We can't see a lick without it," Leena retorted. "But I know these passages well from my kitchen days. The deep cellars are rarely used even by day—it's all specialty rooms this far out. Late at night like now, there's no one about at all."

The firelight flared, which put Juniper to blinking and seeing stars for a good few moments till her vision cleared. Slowly, the passageway took shape around her: narrow and ill-kept, with a packed dirt floor and stone walls dank and stained with moss.

"Is this the dungeon?" Tippy asked, a quaver in her voice.

"No, you goose," said Leena. "Only the food cellars. It gets better looking the farther in you go."

"Oh," said Tippy, clearly underwhelmed.

But Juniper thought it gloriously quaint. "What a place this is!" she breathed. She knew all about the deep cellars, of course—it had been her idea, after all, for Eglantine to unlock this door in particular—but the reality was quite outside her expectations. Knowing *about* these rooms was quite different from walking through them in real and true life.

"Look past the surface and it's a cave of wonders, that's what," said Leena, with some pride. "Only wait till you poke your peepers into some of these rooms. Take this up ahead—one of my favorites. Can you guess?" She nudged Tippy.

Tired though she was, Juniper was curious, too, and now that they were inside the palace, she felt a good deal less anxious. They had a few minutes to explore. She joined the others at the door Leena indicated.

A sharp, moldy smell rose to her nostrils.

"Ewwww!" Tippy whisper-shrieked.

"That's the cheese cave," said Leena proudly. "'Twas my favorite place to work, once upon a day." She waved her torch around to show the tiered wooden shelves topped with large yellow rinds and small mounds wrapped in twine and cheesecloth and thin green-wood strips.

Juniper's stomach growled. Up till now she hadn't really considered cheese beyond its tasteful arrangement on a lunch platter, or the gooey ooze between two crisp slices of toast. But *this* was astonishing! How had it all existed, deep underground, without her ever knowing about it? Then again, she hadn't had much spare time for adventure, back in the day.

As Leena stepped back toward the door, a low rumble echoed through the room. Oona clapped a hand to her belly, looking mortified.

Juniper smiled. "I couldn't agree more. Perhaps we should take a few rounds with us, Leena? We shall need dinner, after all, and I believe we left all our provisions with Root and the horses."

Leena looked unsure, but Juniper was too cheese-happy to care. Making her way down the nearest row, she selected two small wedges that were tucked behind a teetering stack.

After that, they moved more quickly along the corridor. Leena kept up the guided tour but without leading them into any more of the rooms. They passed the mushroom cellar with its musty, earthen tang; the wine cellar, which was barred with a lock the size of Juniper's fist; the cannery, with shelves crowded with jam jars and huge cauldrons waiting above dark fire pits; and the cold-room, which was lined inside with big blocks of ice and hung with preserved and smoked fish and legs of meat. Juniper thought how nicely a strip of smoked underbelly would go with their cheese dinner. But she managed to resist the temptation.

"We're headed somewhere in particular, are we?" Jess asked at last.

"We need somewhere safe to stow away tonight," said Juniper. "Tomorrow, we'll talk about next steps and how we'll manage to find Egg amongst all these halls and spaces."

"Didn't we fly her out a message?" asked Erick.

"Sure, and she left us that door open so we could get in. But the palace is a big place for finding one girl, once you're inside."

"Egg will be the one to find *us*, or I'm no Ceward," said Jess. Again, Juniper noticed an odd sour note to her voice.

"I know just where we can stay," said Leena. She pointed up ahead at a small, nondescript door. "The mudroom—I can't remember the last time this space was used for anything at all. We'll be safe as walls here for the night." She pushed open the door, which swung on its hinges with only a faint creak. One by one they passed through, and Leena shut the door behind them.

Without further delay, Juniper unwrapped the cheeses and broke them into chunks, passing those around, then gobbling down her portion in joyfully creamy mouthfuls. It didn't go far to quenching her hunger, but it would do. For now.

Once the food was gone, the others began dropping down helter-skelter into sleeping spots along the floor. Only Jess took her time, carefully settling Fleeter on her folded cloak, then pulling several jars and bottles out of her skirt and setting about her evening toilette. Juniper herself couldn't get horizontal fast enough: She was tired down to the hollow of her bones. The packed-earth floor was not in the least bit inviting (thankfully, not mud; what *was* the room's name about?). But Juniper's bedding expectations had changed greatly since the Basin. After her long day on horseback, and that mad dash through the grounds, she thought even a bed of nails would have looked inviting.

She bunched up her cloak and made herself as comfortable as she could in her spot on the floor. "We've made it this far," she said as waves of sleep lapped the edges of her mind. "We're inside the walls."

7

AS JESS HAD PROMISED, FINDING HER SISTER
turned out to be as easy as opening their eyes the next morning.

Juniper awoke slowly, taking in the yellow sun filtering through
the narrow sliver of window. They'd slept longer than she'd intended. Then she realized that a noise had awoken her, and she sat
bolt upright.

A girl stood just inside the door, surveying the room and its occu-
pants with an air of quiet interest. Juniper immediately saw the newcomer's resemblance to Jess. So this was the mysterious Eglantine—
or Egg, as Jess called her. She was fine-boned and small enough that
she probably came only up to Juniper's shoulder. Yet Egg was at least
a year older than Jess. Her hair was pulled back from her face in a
tight braid that hung down her back, and her gown with its long,
bell-shaped sleeves was the sort of nondescript color that you forget a
moment after seeing it. No wonder the invaders had underestimated
her! She looked like she couldn't win a butterfight with a squirrel.

Despite her size, though, Egg had a triple dose of presence:

Without even moving a muscle, she looked quietly confident and in full command over the situation. Her eyes were bright and intelligent and, right now, locked unblinkingly on Juniper.

Suddenly remembering that she was in disguise, Juniper scrambled to her feet. "Hullo—Egg, right? I'm Juniper. Princess Juniper—Oh." Of course, Egg was deaf; she couldn't hear a word Juniper was saying. Juniper trailed off, looking over at Jess's still-sleeping form and wishing she were close enough to give the other girl a surreptitious wake-up kick.

Instead, Egg smiled. "I can read your lips," she said, in a clear, careful voice. Her vowels were rounded and her speech halting, but she was easily understandable.

Juniper relaxed immediately, but before she could say anything else, Jess rolled over. Opening her eyes, she took in the scene, then leaped up from her makeshift bedcovers. "It's my Good Egg!" she crowed, then clapped a hand over her mouth as the rest of the kids awoke in a panic.

"I'm sorry—I'm sorry!" panted Jess, looking horrified at her noisy slip. Meanwhile, Egg looked rather smug.

Jess switched to sign language, she and Egg apparently catching each other up on all their adventures so far. After a few minutes, Jess turned back toward the rest of them, while keeping her face angled so Egg could still read her lips.

"So. This is my famous sister, Eglantine, instrumental to getting us back inside these walls."

Egg bobbed her head in greeting. The others waved and nodded and mumbled their hellos.

"As you've seen, Egg can read lips exceptionally well. What that means is if you want her to follow what you're saying, stand where she can see your face. Don't talk over each other; she can't be looking in more than one direction at a time. Also, try not to mumble."

Egg took in Jess's words, then spoke to her sister in sign language, bobbing her head toward the group. "I became deaf in my fourth summer," Jess said, interpreting Egg's signed speech. "This means that even though I'm deaf, I can speak aloud. When I have to." Egg nodded briskly, as though necessary housekeeping was out of the way and now they could get down to business. "I've got a place set up where you can all stay. Up high and out of the way. I've brought some food, too—you must all be hungry."

Jess grinned, signing as she spoke her own words out loud. "Good going, Egg. Surely there's *something* you didn't think of!"

Egg rolled her eyes at the sarcasm, shouldering her taller sister out of the way. Then she nudged her sleeve aside to reveal a patch of coarse, dark fabric strapped to the inside of her arm. Egg fished something out of her pocket—a nub of chalk! She scribbled on the flat of her armband and held it up for them all to see: *Backup*, the word said.

Egg resumed her signing while Jess interpreted. "I can also communicate that way if Jess is not around, though it's slow. Now, we must move before the kitchen gets too busy. I am glad you have come. The danger is mounting, and we have much to do. But first: One of your party is not with you?"

Juniper met Egg's gaze, puzzled. "One of our . . . Well, quite a few of us aren't here now, but—"

Egg gave her head a crisp shake. Furrowing her brow, she gave Jess a fuller explanation in sign language.

Jess's face went pale. "Oh," she said.

"What?" asked Juniper. "Who is she talking about?"

"He's here. In the castle." Jess swallowed. "Cyril Lefarge."

It didn't change anything, not a single thing, Juniper told herself. It wasn't as if they hadn't known Cyril would be coming here. Where else would he have gone? With more than a full day's head start on their travel, of course Cyril would be well settled in by now, bringing his traitorous father up to speed on all the latest developments in Queen's Basin.

Still. It galled Juniper—galled her right down to the gut. To think how she'd trusted that wag-feather! They'd been a *team*. Or, she'd thought they had been.

But none of that mattered any longer. They'd snuck into the palace early, and they would get the jump on Cyril and his backstabbing ways. They were here, lurking and scheming and ready to take him down.

We're coming for you, Cyril, Juniper thought. *Just you wait!*

The first step was to get to the hideaway. Egg described it briefly, signing while Jess interpreted. Juniper could have hugged Egg. "You're talking about the Aerie!" she said.

The others looked confused, so Juniper explained: "You know our little messenger? Those ghost bats my father breeds, which deliver our letters? He set up a special loft for their living quarters and took on every aspect of their training and care himself. I wondered what would become of them when he was made captive." She paused while Jess finished signing her words to Egg, who grinned and flashed her own reply.

"The bats are well," she said. "I have been taking care of them."

Juniper felt something squeeze inside her chest. "Both my father and I are indebted to you, Egg."

"All right," said Jess, though she didn't stop signing. "It's just what needed doing, I'm sure. Now, if we've had enough speechifying, maybe we can pack ourselves off to this hideaway? Before the kitchen decides on mushroom mash for dinner and we are caught out cold."

With no further prompting, the kids scurried around the room, straightening and tidying anything they had touched and removing all trace of their presence. Tippy tried to pick up Fleeter, but Jess refused, insisting he would stay properly quiet only for her. Then, after a last look around to be sure all was in order, Juniper and Egg led the way out into the cellar corridor.

At the foot of the long staircase up to the back kitchens, Juniper said, "The palace is riddled with secret rooms and back passages. It was a hobby of mine growing up to find as many as I could. Pockets, I call them, and they're pretty much all connected." She paused while Jess caught up with her sign language interpretation, then went on. "I can get us to the Aerie using them and staying altogether out of sight—*but* first we have to reach the entry point."

"Where is that?" asked Tippy.

"The nearest is up these stairs and down the hall. Not too far, but it's in the pantry—and we've got to go through the back kitchen to get there."

Leena widened her eyes at this.

"What?" asked Oona.

"The kitchens are sure to be all aflutter this time of day. 'Twould be on any old day—we're coming up near noontime, if I'm not mistaken—but with the Summerfest so soon?" She shook her head.

It was true. Even from this far down, they could hear the rattle of banging pots, clomping feet, and barking voices. How on earth were they going to get to the Pockets without being seen?

"I can cause a distraction," Egg said, signing a more lengthy explanation to Jess and then marching up the steps.

Of course. Egg didn't have to remain hidden.

"Come on," said Jess. "Egg will act quickly, so let's all be ready to bolt when she does."

Juniper wished she could call her thanks to Egg for so quickly taking charge, but the girl's back was already turned as she sped up the cellar stairs. Juniper grabbed Jess's arm. "What is the sign for 'thank you'?"

Jess raised her flat hand to her lips and brought it out and slightly down, almost like she was blowing a kiss but without moving her lips. She gave a nod as Juniper copied her, then said, "Come on. There'll be time for sign lessons later."

At the top of the stairs, Egg pushed the door and stepped through, leaving it cracked open behind her. The others were already partway up the stairs, and Juniper hurried after them. From the hallway they heard a slip and then a shriek—not Egg's—and then a clamor of voices and stamping feet heading away down the hall.

The others paused at the door, and Erick peeked around the side of it. He waved a hand vigorously back at them, and they all scurried up the rest of the way. The coast was clear!

Through the corridor they flitted, then into the emptied-out back kitchen. There, a whisk still vibrated slightly in a bowl of fluff; a pot bubbled merrily on the stovetop; an enormous loaf of bread lay half sliced and steaming hot on the countertop. Despite the rush, Juniper couldn't help reaching out and snatching one of the middle slices from the loaf, then nudging the rest back into shape around it. How she had missed the rich, nutty warmth of fresh-baked bread! Then they were through to the far side of the room, where the kitchen opened into the pantry.

They just had to make it through here and—

"I don't know what to do with that girl," came Cook's blustering voice from the hall—just up ahead and moving fast in their direction. "She goes about all quiet and innocent-like, but I could swear there's more to her than . . ."

Juniper looked wildly around. The six of them had made it into the walk-through pantry, and Juniper could see the trapdoor grate that led to the nearest Pocket—a small holding room behind the kitchen walls.

But they had no time.

Dashing to the edge of the room, she whipped open the grate and pushed Tippy inside. Jess followed close behind, then Oona, then Erick. Leena was nowhere to be seen, and Juniper spent a frantic second scanning the room, unable to call out under the rapidly approaching footsteps, until she saw that Leena had ducked behind a bag of flour nearly as large as she was. This was clearly a room the girl knew well.

Juniper turned back to the grate, only to nearly jump out of her skin at a voice just around the corner.

"Melody!" Cook bellowed. "Get you in here sharpish!"

In the last half second before Cook rounded the doorway, Juniper flattened herself against the far wall covering the grate, pulling her snow-white cloak tight around her and yanking the hood low over her face. Then she held her breath and made herself perfectly immobile in the gloomy half-light.

Cook blew through the pantry, still yelling for her helper. Without so much as a glance around, she vanished into the kitchen.

Juniper let her breath out in a whoosh. She knew that Cook had just been distracted—why should she be on the alert for stray princesses in her pantry, after all? But a small, secret part of Juniper couldn't help remembering what Mother Odessa had said when she'd given the cloak as a parting gift. It had been Juniper's mother's cloak, and when she'd worn it, Odessa had said, she'd always felt invincible. Odessa had given Juniper a bright blue stone, too, which she squeezed now in a silent pulse of thanks.

If there was any strength to be drawn from the ghosts of the past, Juniper thought, she was open and ready.

With the pantry empty once again, Juniper and Leena ducked inside the secret trapdoor, reuniting with the rest of the gang in the Pocket behind the kitchen. Their destination—the Aerie— was clear on the other side of the palace, and several stories up to boot. Egg was long gone, presumably on her way there through the regular aboveboard channels. But Juniper knew these Pockets like the back of her hand. She quickly plotted a map in her head and led the others from one dark, narrow space to another. Sometimes they had to turn sideways to fit through cramped cubbies and around tight turns. A few times they had to get down on all fours and crawl.

Partway along, the gasps and wheezes from behind Juniper—not to mention her own constricting chest—made her wave her hand in the universal gesture for *Let's take a break, all!* She knew they were up on the living quarters floor, which should be mostly empty, but she didn't want to risk speaking aloud. With a finger to her lips in the half-light, Juniper crept toward the wall of their narrow hiding spot. There was a peephole at about shoulder height. Through the tiny gap she could see one of the palace's dozens of guest rooms, impeccably made-up but clearly unoccupied, with dust covers draping all the visible furniture.

Good. They could talk without fear of being overheard.

"We need to split up for a bit," said Juniper in a low voice, leaning in close to the others. "You can easily reach the Aerie by following this wall-ladder up, then just scooting along that passage to its end. When in doubt, go higher. But I've got a stop I want to make first. Erick—will you come with me?"

Erick gladly agreed, while the others seemed content to head for the Aerie. Only Tippy looked torn between staying with Juniper and wanting to try out her climbing skills on the metal prongs arranged into a makeshift ladder leading straight up the wall. The wall-stair won, as Juniper had figured it would. She wondered if Tippy, too, was thinking of the Climbing Tree back at the Anju village. For a moment Juniper was distracted by the thought of someday making her very own climbing area, right here on the palace grounds. Why not?

Then she briskly boxed that idea away. There would be time for recreational improvements in future, but that time was *not* now. Securing the palace was her only goal. Everything else would have to wait.

Juniper and Erick turned right, and the others turned left.

"So where are we heading exactly?" Erick whispered as they scrambled around a corner and pushed farther into the second-floor Pockets.

"We'll hear all about what's going on in the palace, just as soon as we can get the full story from Egg. But first there's someone—" She shook her head. "Some*place* I just have to see."

"Your father?" said Erick. "But how—"

"They'd have him locked up in his rooms, wouldn't they?" Juniper's heart was thundering in her chest now. She was surprised Erick couldn't hear it. "And the Royal Suite has more Pockets than a billiard table. If we can get the lay of the land in there, we'll be able to spirit him out in no time."

8

THE ROYAL SUITE TOOK UP THE WHOLE SOUTH wing of the castle. The best-situated peephole—and the largest—looked out from the main sitting room's fireplace. Thankfully it was summertime, so the hearth wasn't in use and they could spy in safety.

This room was the largest in the Royal Suite. It was crammed with bookshelves, balconies, comfortable seating nooks, and even a large harpsichord. The ceiling arched high overhead in a flare of brightly painted frescoes. It had always been her father's favorite place to relax, and the nearer they got, the more Juniper's mind was flooded with moments they had shared within its walls.

Creeping along in the darkness now, a world and more away from that one, Juniper pressed her palms hard into the walls as she passed them. *Keep it steady,* she told herself. *One foot in front of the other. Sneak and stealth are what will win this fight.*

As they approached the suite, Juniper could hear the sound of raised voices echoing through the Pockets. Her pulse skyrocketed, but the next moment, it plummeted to the depths. This was not the authoritative rumble of her father's voice. Nor was it the deferential murmur of guards on duty.

One voice was sharp, strident, and female. The other voice was familiar as an old toothache: It belonged to Cyril.

Of course it did.

"—long has he been like this?" Cyril's voice was tight with anger.

The eyehole was set low on the wall—barely thigh-high—and Juniper had to crouch on the dusty floorboards to reach it. She scooted over to make room for Erick next to her. Looking through the long, narrow slit, Juniper could see Cyril's legs and tall, pointy-toed boots (polished to a glossy sheen, obviously), set wide apart on the carpet. He stood directly in front of her father's favorite stuffed armchair. Someone was sitting there—someone who was *not* King Regis. But who *was* it? All Juniper could see was a waterfall of silk skirts pooling across the floor.

"Cyril. Dear boy." The woman's voice was all honeysome now, the kind of overwrought ooze that made Juniper shudder on Cyril's behalf—and she didn't even like him anymore. Who *was* this creep occupying her father's chair and outvillaining their number one villain? And what had been done with her father? This mission to locate him had been a failure, but now that they were here, she had to stay and find out more.

The woman went on: "Your father just needs *time* and *rest*. Your absence on that jaunt of yours has been a blessing, truly. The dear man hasn't had to worry about a thing." A powdered white hand stretched languidly out and hung quivering in space for a bare second before a maid scurried over, nearly tripping in her haste. The maid wedged a porcelain teacup into the hollow of the woman's open hand. Cup was brought leisurely to lips.

Good grief!

"Hasn't had to worry?" Cyril stormed. "My father is delirious. He's been sick abed for weeks! It seems to me that *we* should be worrying about *him*."

"I've secured the very best care for dearest Rupert after his accident. You know this. The physician has been tending him twice daily, and I myself *leap* to his every need." The hand wafted out again. The maid darted over with a faint gasp and caught the teacup just as the pale hand opened carelessly to let it go. The skirts rustled as the armchair diva let out a long-suffering sigh. "You *do* trust me, don't you, Cyril dear? After all these years together?"

Of course. Details clicked in Juniper's mind, and she knew who the impostor was. From the quick intake of breath, Juniper knew Erick had just made the same connection. "It's Cyril's stepmother," he mouthed.

Juniper nodded, her mind racing. Malvinia Lefarge was the wife of Rupert, her father's chief adviser and the man whose betrayal had first let the Monsians breach Torr Castle. Now it sounded like Rupert himself was badly sick and out of action—at least temporarily. This could be good news for their efforts!

But the question still remained: Why was Cyril's stepmother in the king's chambers?

Juniper had met Malvinia Lefarge only a few times. She was

a rigid, supercilious woman who spent most of her time in her northern mansion, visiting the palace only for parties and grand occasions of state, even though her husband lived here year-round. Yet she now seemed very much settled and at home in the royal chambers.

Alta and Jess had warned them that the Lefarges had taken over the rule of Torr. Apparently, that included taking over the ruler's living quarters, too.

Back inside the sitting room, Cyril gave a little snort. "You're changing the subject," he said.

His stepmother's voice hardened. "Maybe the subject needs further changing. What have *you* been up to these many weeks? Your father and I were assured of receiving regular letters and reports of what you learned while away. But I saw no such missives."

Juniper knew Cyril had intended to spy on her for his father, but it still stung to hear it said aloud. She saw Cyril's hands clench, but all he said was, "As you might imagine, Stepmother, my means of communication were limited. I have a full report ready to be delivered to my father." He paused meaningfully. "Just as soon as he is awake and on his feet again."

Malvinia sighed. "I have no idea what game you're playing at, Cyril. But surely you have *some* information you can convey to me in the meanwhile. You see that I'm doing my best to keep things running while your father is indisposed. Tell me you managed at least to notice in what condition you left the former princess. Does she know what has gone on here?"

Now it was Juniper's turn to ball her hands into fists. *Former* princess?! Oh, if she could just topple this dividing wall and pop both traitors a roundhouse kick to the jaw! Why, oh, why hadn't they managed to cow Cyril before he got back to the palace? He might not know their up-to-date plans, but he still knew so much.

Cyril's response was breezy, and he started pacing the room again. "Ah, you know our flighty little Juniper. She is aware of the transition, in broad strokes, though how much she cares in the long run is hard to say. I shouldn't be surprised if she moves her puny group to attempt some little skirmish back here, but I should not worry on that overmuch."

"Hmm," said Malvinia noncommittally. "Has she plans to return this way, then?"

"Well, the last I heard—"

Suddenly, there was a light creak behind Juniper, then a pair of small hands grabbed her eyes. "Guess who?!" The whispered words in Juniper's ear were scarcely above a breath, but coming unexpectedly as they did, Juniper toppled headfirst into the peephole, mashing her nose badly and seeing stars for a good few seconds.

"Gadzooks!" came Tippy's low gasp behind her. The little girl's yen for mischief was legendary, but this was going too far!

While Juniper struggled to pull herself together, Erick swept Tippy up and dragged her bodily, though stealthily, back down the corridor. Tippy wrung her hands and made small flaps of apology, but Juniper's full attention was on the other side of that wall. Tippy's murmur was near inaudible, but Juniper herself had fallen hard. Could they have heard?

Faint with dread, clutching her throbbing nose, Juniper eased back to the peephole. The room had gone silent, the former conversation abandoned.

"Did you hear—" Malvinia began.

Then Cyril said, "Oh, Artie, not again!" He turned toward the doorway that led farther into the suite. His stepmother stood with an exasperated sigh and strode past him across the room, her skirts swishing in her wake. The maid scurried at her heels. A moment later, Juniper could hear a strange sort of—muttering? cooing? what *was* that sound?—coming from the far chamber.

Alone in the sitting room, Cyril stuck his hands in his pockets. He paced the room, turning in a full circle and then coming to stand directly in front of the fireplace that was her hiding spot. For several long heartbeats, they stood, each one motionless on their own side of the brick façade. Juniper wished the viewing slit weren't set so low, that she could see his expression and have some sense of what might be going through his head.

Could he suspect?

Then Cyril let out his breath and kept moving. A few moments later, he followed Malvinia into the far chamber. The door shut behind him with a click.

Knees cramped and aching, Juniper tottered to her feet. She backed slowly down the narrow passageway and made her escape.

9

"THAT WAS *TOO* CLOSE A CALL," SAID JUNIPER.
Even now, a full half hour later, her fingers trembled faintly. If
Malvinia or Cyril *had* heard—well. The Pockets weren't exactly
a palace secret. They were impractical for the servants to bother
with, and too uncomfortable for the average grown-up. Juniper
herself had noticed that the ceilings and walls were a lot closer than
they'd been a few months ago, and lanky Leena looked like a black-
bird squeezing into a wedge of pie. No, they wouldn't be tripping
over any rogue palace staff inside the Pockets.

But if there was ever any sign of intruders, that would be a different story. The Pockets, then, would be the first place searched.
Once the hunt began, it would quickly end in discovery, and that
would mean imprisonment for the lot of them. Bam! Their mission
would be over before it began.

Juniper's shoulders slumped. Her nose felt bruised and mushy.

Next to her, Tippy hiccupped loudly.

"You'd no cause to come barreling after us like that, Tippy," said Erick. This was just the tail end of a lecture that had been going on for some time. "You could have banjaxed everything."

"I'm awfully sorry," Tippy whispered. Her cheeks were wet, and her collar looked damp and sticky. "I was being ever so stealthy—not a sound nor a word said I! But I couldn't stay away. It's just, what if you needed me to save the day? And I never bothered to come?"

Juniper ruffled the little girl's hair. "There, Tipster. Buck up," she said. She sent a lopsided grin Erick's way. "We won't say any more about it. Only, after you've thought a plan through next time, think on it twice and thrice again, all right? This is a dangerous game we're playing."

"It's not a *game* at all," said Jess acidly. "But enough of this water dribbling. We all need to know what you two saw and heard down there."

"Yes!" said Oona. "Did you find the king?"

Juniper shook her head. She looked around the assembled group at the Aerie. The room was much the same as the last time she'd been here with her father to check on the health of one of his ailing ghost bats. The wide round space filled the peak of the highest palace turret. Tall, gleaming windows encircled the whole room, filling it with light and giving a magnificent view of the castle grounds. Below the north-side windows was a bank of tiny straw-filled cubbyhole-nests, with a half dozen pale winged creatures tucked away inside. Because this room had been a favorite spot of the king's—his private getaway nook, as well as his bat cave—the section of room apart from the animals had comfortable couches and one hairy sheep-pelt rug, a low rustic table, a porcelain washing basin, and a heap of pillows. (King Regis dearly loved pillows.) Now the bats were humming in their dens, a fresh pitcher of water lay beading on the table, and—as Egg had promised—a heaping bowl of fruit and nuts overflowed alongside.

Judging by the neat pile of belongings stacked in an empty wooden crate, it seemed that Egg had been living here for some time. Juniper noted with interest a tall bow and quiver of arrows propped against the couch. Another of the mysterious Egg's skills, no doubt.

Over the steady sound of munching, Juniper relayed who was now occupying her father's suite, and the conversation they'd overheard. Jess had sat them all in a circle where they would be easily visible to Egg, and kept up a running sign language interpretation. Egg nodded at intervals to show she was following.

"And that's the long and short of it," Juniper concluded. "Cut off by . . ." She waved a hand vaguely.

Tippy ducked her head. She reached to stroke the patchy mottle of Fleeter's fur, where he lay sprawled on a plump mustard-colored pillow. He was sound asleep. Did that cat do anything but sleep? At least he had shown no interest in chasing the bats, which would have been a trial.

"Something caught their attention, just at the opportune moment," Erick cut in, shifting the focus from Tippy's error.

"So what was it they ran off after?" asked Leena.

"Oh, I can tell you that," said Jess airily, though Juniper noticed that Egg had first started moving her hands to contribute.

Seeing Jess, the older girl settled back on her pillow, her eyes flashing bright. Jess said, "Rupert and Malvinia Lefarge have a small offspring."

That took the wind out of Juniper's sails. "They have *what*? A child, quite aside from Cyril?"

"How can that be?" Erick asked. "Lady Malvinia has not lived at the castle with her husband for several years."

Egg tilted her head in Juniper's direction.

"Egg?" Juniper said.

"It is a little boy," Jess said while Egg signed. "About three years old. Malvinia Lefarge first retired from court upon her confinement and never fully returned after the child was born."

"Until now," said Oona, frowning.

Come to think of it, Malvinia had been quite a fixture at court some . . . four years ago. Huh. So that was why she'd disappeared: to have a child. But— "Cyril, a big brother?" She shook her head. "I just can't picture it."

"Well, that's paltry enough information we've got, to be sure," said Jess, her hands flashing like quicksilver. "It's impossible to predict which of our secrets that rat would have spilled right before your eyes if they weren't interrupted."

"I think it's safe to assume that anything and everything he knows about our plans will come out eventually," said Juniper.

"It seemed to me . . ." said Erick, shifting on the floor to tuck his legs underneath him. "Juniper, did you get a sense that he didn't much care for his stepmother?"

"Definitely," Juniper agreed. "I bet he's saving the real juicy information to give directly to his father, once he's on the mend." She brightened. "So it could be we have a little more time. There's some tension between those two, for sure. Cyril's holding out on her. *And* he thinks we're not coming back into the palace for another week."

Leena nodded. "He thinks he can afford to wait."

"We can't take anything for granted," said Erick. "But it is some relief."

"We'll need to keep our eyes on him," said Jess. "As much as ever we can. The moment he finks on us, we'll need to know it."

"And anything else he's up to along the way," said Oona.

"More important than any of this, though," Juniper interrupted, "is locating the king. Remember: All we have to do is free him. Then the whole jig is up."

"*All* we have to do," said Leena, half under her breath.

"About the king," said Egg, through Jess, "I don't know." Her face was crimson, as though the admission gave her physical pain.

"It's all right to not know things sometimes, Egg," Jess said, but her tone had a slight edge.

Erick cleared his throat. Then he was silent so long that the others all turned to stare at him.

"What?" Juniper said.

"I don't know how to put this," he said, picking at a thread in the silky pillow on his lap. "But do we know for sure that, um, King Regis is still—"

He couldn't say any more; he didn't need to. Juniper felt her heart go still in her chest. She was unable to answer him.

Instead, Egg shook her head so firmly that her braid whipped around and smacked her on the cheek. Through Jess, she said, "King Regis *is* alive. He is in the dungeon. I meant only that I have not been in there myself, to see him. I do not know exactly where or how he is imprisoned."

Juniper found she could breathe again. "Well," she managed. "This is good. We know he is safe at least."

"If you can call it that," said Jess.

"I'm sorry," said Erick. "I didn't mean to . . ." But he looked no less shaken than she was at the prospect of the dungeons. As captain of the guard, his own father would be locked up right along with the king—and countless other parents and family members, including Tippy's beloved older sister, Elly.

"It's all right," said Juniper. "So, the king is in the dungeons. And there are no Pockets down there." Juniper's pulse still felt jittery, and she forced herself to breathe. Just free her father—that was all they had to do! And then he could take control. That would fix everything.

But *how?*

"We should set up a spying rotation," said Oona timidly, "like we did back at the Basin with guard duty."

"A guard duty, but for information gathering," said Juniper. "I like it."

"Spying duty!" said Tippy. She shook her hair in front of her face as though she were hiding behind a bush, and flashed her hands out wide. "Look: spy hands!"

"All right, let's get organized," said Juniper. "There's ever so much to be done. We need eyes on Malvinia and on Lefarge himself, sick though he may be. On Cyril, for sure. We need to know exactly what nobles and dignitaries are in the palace and where they are staying. And whatever we can learn about the dungeons—guards, servants, layout, anything at all. Any way we can get my father out of there." Juniper looked up, catching Erick's eye. "And the other prisoners, of course. Basically, we need to know what we're up against. The one thing we lack here is information."

"Do you?" asked Egg aloud.

Juniper blinked. What was it Jess had said when they were back in the Basin? The Monsians had not imprisoned Egg—despite her being older than a fair few footmen and serving girls across the palace—because they'd underestimated her. Juniper had scoffed at this, yet hadn't she herself done the same thing? She looked Egg in the eyes, took in her intelligence, the sharp wit that lay behind her tiny frame and measured speech. Egg wouldn't push herself forward, Juniper suddenly knew. She had no desire to flaunt her own might; if she was not relied on, she would simply go about her own business, taking all her skills and know-how with her. But if she was truly brought in as part of the team . . . Juniper thought Egg might be very valuable indeed. She'd already more than proven this.

"All right, then. Egg," said Juniper, "you've been right here in the soup, so to speak, and I can see that you've been paying attention. What do you have to share with us about the state of affairs in Torr Castle?"

· · ·

With Jess as interpreter, Egg's information came out in full and careful detail. Cyril's stepmother, Malvinia Lefarge, while being Torrean born and bred, apparently had blood ties to Monsia. In fact, she was a distant cousin of the Scion of Monsia himself. Rupert Lefarge's first wife—Cyril's mother—had died in childbirth, and he had married Malvinia some years later. According to Egg's sources (Juniper would have given a lot to know who or what they were!), the woman had taken yearly pilgrimages to a hot springs colony on Spyglass Lake in northern Torr. Only, it turned out that for well over a decade she had not been traveling to Spyglass Lake at all. Instead, she had been sneaking into Monsia, to reacquaint herself with her distant family.

"It would seem that her many-times-great-grandmother performed some invaluable service for the then Scion of Monsia," Jess said. "And she was granted a Golden Bequest."

"A golden whatsit?" asked Tippy.

Erick's face lit up at this sliver of history brought into the real world. "Golden Bequest," he said. His fingers twitched as though turning imaginary book pages. "It's an ancient Monsian custom—virtually unknown in these times. It is a wish to be granted by the Scion of Monsia to one of his subjects—anything at all within his power. Only think of it!"

Egg nodded, continued signing, and Jess carried on the narrative out loud. "That relative having perished with the grant still unused, the Golden Bequest became lost to history. Until Malvinia uncovered written evidence of it in her research of her family tree."

From Malvinia's view, the plan had been simple. She and her husband, Rupert Lefarge, had conspired for nothing less than the throne of Torr. Their Bequest (for the throne of Torr was clearly not Monsia's to give) brought in the support of the Monsian army to secure the overthrow.

And now here they were.

"So," said Erick thoughtfully, "the Lefarges are behind the takeover, and not Monsia directly."

"Is there any real difference, when it comes down to the fact?" said Juniper. "If they've got Monsia's support, then it's Monsia we're coming against. The castle is crawling with their soldiers, after all."

"What baffles me is how this moldy old something-or-other promise would be enough to take a whole kingdom to war. Who could think it?" said Jess.

"I don't know how much encouragement was necessary to bring the Monsians against us," said Juniper. "I should imagine that the promise of a traitor opening our impregnable gates would be lure enough. But tell me more about Lefarge himself, Egg. He is taken out sick, we heard?"

Egg nodded and began signing, while Jess interpreted. "Rupert Lefarge had a riding accident some weeks ago. He hasn't regained consciousness since. Word around the palace is that the fall might have brought on a brain fever. In his absence, Malvinia is in charge."

"Well, that's a good thing, then, isn't it?" said Leena. "We have the stepmother at the helm—a backup traitor rather than the real true original."

"How *is* she managing the kingdom?" asked Juniper. There was something in what she'd seen of Malvinia's bearing, her speech, that did not feel quite—how could she put it?—did not feel quite like "backup" material. This was not a lady, she suspected, who liked taking orders from anybody.

Egg frowned at Juniper's question, and her hands started moving again. Jess went on: "She is . . . distracted. At first she spent most of her time in the sickroom caring for Lefarge. But increasingly she has gone about running the castle and catching up on affairs of state. She is . . ."

Egg brought her hands together. "Very capable," she said aloud. She tapped the side of her head and gave a small shiver. "Smart. Too smart, maybe."

At this, Juniper sat up straight. Egg seemed almost more intimidated by Malvinia than by Lefarge. Could things be even worse than Juniper had suspected? Had they gone from the kettle into the fire?

"We need a code name," Juniper decided.

The others looked up, puzzled. "For Malvinia?" asked Oona.

Jess nodded. "I agree. We should say her name out loud as little as possible."

Juniper looked at Tippy, who clapped in delight. "Oh, I do love me a nickname!" Then she knit her brows while the others waited. At last she said, "Don't she look a bit like a praying mantis, though?

Spindly arms like claws drawn up at her front, and ready to sort of munch down on anyone who gets in her way?"

This brought a round of hearty laughter, but Juniper loved it. "Malvinia the Mantis. That's just right! The Mantis it is."

With this decided, the group began plotting in earnest. In the end, they pooled their knowledge to reach the following conclusions:

• Aside from the charred fields (according to Egg, Malvinia had been furious at this destruction), the Monsians had not pushed their invasion beyond the castle walls. So the Queen's Basin team didn't have to worry about enemy troops running around the rest of Torr, which was a relief.

• Several battalions of Monsian soldiers were on-site and on duty in Torr Castle, but the day-to-day running of the palace was fully in the hands of the Lefarges. Thus, their battle was currently a hostile takeover, not an enemy invasion—a difference that was subtle, but critical.

• With Rupert out of action, the one in charge (for now, at least) was Malvinia alone.

"So this is truly our best window for action," said Erick, pulling a book onto his lap and stroking its spine lovingly. "Right now, the Monsian presence is small, led by a single leader, and so more vulnerable to our counterattack."

"Right *now*," said Jess. "But when will reinforcements come?"

"Soon," said Egg.

"That's right," Juniper agreed. "We already know they are on the way, for my father is to be taken to Monsia by the end of Summerfest. That will be when they sweep in with the rest of their army, lock down the palace, and begin enacting the next stage of their mayhem." She looked around the circle. "Torr is safe for now, but by the end of next week—who can say?"

Cyril's role in all this remained uncertain. How much would he get involved with his father's and stepmother's nefarious schemes? How fierce an enemy would he prove to be? From personal experience, Juniper knew what lengths Cyril could leap to when he wanted something.

But what did he want, exactly?

Another important factor: Across the palace, Malvinia Lefarge was widely disliked. Most of the longtime palace staff and guards had been locked up in the dungeons below the palace. The Torrean army had been replaced with Monsian soldiers and rogue swords-for-hire, but the new palace workers were mostly townsfolk from Torrence and other nearby villages, who took the opportunity to gain a cushy palace job in exchange for swearing a loyalty oath to the interlopers.

"Dirty traitors," growled Erick, in an uncharacteristic display of anger.

Juniper felt much the same, but Jess cut him off smoothly. "They have to survive, like anyone," she said. "However these traitorous rulers came to their power, they *are* now in command. We can't blame folks for taking the opportunities handed to them."

"Can't we, though?" Juniper jumped in. "Do you really think these lowlifes could stay in control if there were no maids or cooks or floor scrubbers or bottle washers to keep the palace upright around them?" She felt her cheeks heat as she said this; a month ago, had she even known what it took to keep a kingdom running, even a small one like this palace? But all she'd learned in building and ruling Queen's Basin was deep within her now. No, she couldn't completely blame the poor workers who had been drawn over to what seemed the winning side. But she didn't think they were blameless, either.

"Still," said Erick, his voice level again and the flush of anger gone from his cheeks, "this is good for us on the whole. Lily-livers or not, these new palace workers are all Torrean citizens."

"Yes," said Leena. "They might have sworn some fool oath, but that doesn't mean we can't win them back to our side—or bring out their true colors if they feel safe enough to display them."

"Everyone hates her," said Egg, moving her hands in a broad gesture.

"That's a good starting point," said Juniper. "It's something we can use. Now we just need to get the rest of the way there. Get us in—and her *out*. Save the king and liberate the castle."

How to Overthrow a Palace When You Are Understaffed, Underarmed, and Underaged

#1: Know your enemy.

It pays to know all you can about who you are fighting. *Why* is important, but *what* is essential. What are their habits, routines, or rituals? What do they like and what do they hate? The more you know, the more there is to exploit.

#2: Sweat the small stuff.

Your goal might be huge, but the best way to get there is with small steps. Keep an eye out for little ways to wreak your havoc. The tallest walls are built brick by brick—and they can be toppled the same way.

#3: Await your moment.

The difference between the right time to move and the wrong one is the difference between a safe walk over the bridge and a dunking into the stream. Go slow enough to pay attention; when the right time comes, you'll know it.

#4: When the time is right, be bold.

Once that moment is reached, pounce! Don't hesitate. Don't look back. Don't second-guess. You've come this far on sheer guts and gumption. Ride the force of that wave all the way through to the victorious finish.

10

DESPITE ALL THEIR KNUCKLE GNAWING—OR
perhaps *because* of it, taking Oona's view of the helpful powers of
worrying—there was no visible fallout from the kerfuffle outside
the Royal Suite. Neither Cyril nor his stepmother gave any sense
of knowing they had been spied upon. Gradually, Team Goshawk
relaxed. Over the next few days, they settled into a sort of routine.
(Juniper considered making a schedule, but decided that might be a
bit over-the-top, even for her.) They rose early, divided into scouting groups, and spent their days lurking in the Pockets, spying on
the palace from inside the walls. At night, they met in the Aerie
and pooled their information, which Erick transcribed onto one
extra-large roll of parchment, which they set out on the low table as
a sort of master spy document. (It was nearly as good as a schedule,
come to think of it.)

Egg's assessment of the staff had been right-on: To Malvinia's
face, every person was courteous, attentive, and perfectly behaved.

But she just had to leave the room for the frowns and mutterings to start up.

Surely the Queen's Basin team could exploit this, when the time was right.

Rupert Lefarge stayed unresponsive in his sick room, his condition unchanged. A serving boy came in to spoon-feed him sugar water and thick broth several times a day. Cyril continued to hold his information close, ignoring his stepmother's questions and spending a great deal of time at his father's bedside, or—uncharacteristically, Juniper thought, given his self-absorbed nature—taking his young half brother on energetic runs in the palace gardens or reading him piles of brightly colored picture books.

Nobles and dignitaries arrived daily from all over Torr and beyond, settling into the guest wing suites in preparation for the upcoming Summerfest. The staff worked flat-out from morning till night. So many of the longtime members had chosen imprisonment rather than pledging loyalty to the new rulers that the palace was seriously understaffed. And those who were at work were mostly new and untrained. According to Leena, it would take a miracle for them to pull off the big Summerfest banquet.

The most important piece of information, however, was the single one they had not been able to verify: No one had yet made it into the dungeon to lay eyes on King Regis.

"I've gone as near as I dared and spied through the closest Pocket for hours," said Jess. "The guards are vigilant and relentless."

"We have to find a way in there," said Erick. "Freeing the king is the key to everything."

But the dungeon was locked up tight as a drum, with a strict rotation and no fewer than three guards at the entrance. No one outside the elite guard contingent was allowed inside the reinforced doors. Extra guards came to carry food trays, waiting outside the door to provide support until the front guards returned with the empty dishes.

The only other known set of keys was kept in the one place they could not access: on a thick ring securely fastened around the Mantis's waist.

"I'm officially making this our primary goal," Juniper told the group. "We have *got* to find a way to get into the dungeon!"

With the prisoners frustratingly out of reach, Juniper wedged herself into the spying rotation by spending a good chunk of time in Rupert Lefarge's sickroom. The only peephole was in the anteroom, and Juniper could see only a small bit of the bedchamber from her spot in the Pockets. But it was enough to watch Cyril make his way there early in the morning, take a seat next to his father's still form, and keep up a patter of one-way conversation across the hours that Juniper kept her quiet vigil. At one point, Cyril disappeared for more than an hour, coming back with a bowlful of something pungent that curled her toes and made her eyes water from clear across the suite. This he slowly and painstakingly spooned into his father's mouth.

What on earth was Cyril doing?

Aside from those gag-inducing minutes, the chamber was mostly still, and time passed uneventfully. Near the end of the day, when Juniper's legs were cramped and her back ached something fierce, a loud *rat-a-tat* came on the door of Lefarge's room, which then exploded open in a whirl of small-bodied frenzy.

So this was the little mystery boy.

"Ceepee! Papa?" he lisped, throwing himself at the end of the bed.

"Come on, Artie, you know Papa's sleeping," said Cyril, in a low voice. Unreasonably, Juniper wanted the kid to keep shouting. I mean, if someone's in an unconscious sleep, that's a bad thing, right? Why *wouldn't* you want the kind of loud noise that might wake him up?

Still, Cyril evidently didn't see it that way, for he gathered the little tyke in a playful headlock and zoomed him out of the room. The door shut behind them. Juniper listened to the stuttered breathing of her father's former chief adviser for several long minutes. Then she sighed, creaked to a standing position, and headed back for the Aerie.

Pulling herself up through the trapdoor in the middle of the floor, Juniper found Egg standing alone at a window, looking out over the grounds. Unsure how to make the girl aware of her presence, Juniper walked up and touched Egg on the shoulder. The other girl just nodded like she'd known Juniper was there already.

Without Jess around to interpret, Egg hiked up her sleeve to reveal her armband and fished out her chalk. "Wood floors," she wrote. "You walk like a draco."

"I do not!" said Juniper indignantly, then she giggled. "I prefer to think I move like a draco in *flight*, all grace and glory."

She flapped her arms out like wings, and Egg rolled her eyes.

"I've ridden one, you know. A live draco. No, really." She could see that Egg didn't believe her. "People think they're just beasts of legend, but there's at least one in the world that's as live as you or I. It's a stout friend—never say a pet!—of my blood sister, Zetta, the ruler of the Anju."

"Blood sister? What is that?"

"Oh, she's not a proper sister. It goes deeper than that, a blood bond that extends to the heart of the Lower Continent itself." Juniper turned toward the window, then caught herself and faced back toward Egg, hoping she was forming the words distinctly enough. She knew lipreading was not easy work. "I don't truly understand it all myself. It's something I wish to learn more about from the Anju someday."

"You fought the Anju, yes?"

"Not exactly," said Juniper. "It's . . . complicated. My mother was born Anju and was to be their chief, ever so long back. When we came upon them in the Hourglass Mountains some weeks ago, they were holding trials to choose their next chief. For a time, I thought that if I could become their leader, it would gain me a fighting force against the Monsians."

Egg raised a quizzical brow.

"Well, good intentions don't pave roads," Juniper said. "I was wrong to force myself on them, but it worked out in the end. We're all friends now, and I ended up with something better than subjects: allies."

"And the draco?"

"Who knows what he's up to? Lumbering about his cave, no doubt."

Egg seemed to be digesting this whole exchange. She fumbled with her chalk a bit, erasing and rewriting a couple times before angling her arm for Juniper to see. "Your experience is interesting. But I have found self-reliance the best guarantee of success."

This surprised Juniper. "Oh, you can't think that! How can one person be and do everything that's needed?"

Egg shrugged. "A true spy stands alone." Then her head turned to follow a movement in the gardens. "I must go," she wrote. She turned and grabbed her bow and arrow from the couch, then headed down the stairs.

Long after she left, Juniper stood gazing out over the grounds, watching the group of young nobles clustered around the archery targets. Egg had joined them in her most innocent pose, obviously trying to blend in and continue her surreptitious information gathering. Farther out beyond the palace peaks and gables and tiled turrets stretched the White Highway, and farther still—oh, so unreachably far away—were Juniper's beloved Hourglass Mountains. Somewhere nestled in them lay Queen's Basin, her tiny mountain kingdom just awaiting her return. And on its neighboring peak was the Anju village, which had carved such a deep spot into her heart. How could she have begun to tell Egg how the Anju trials had bonded Zetta and her for life? How could she have expressed the feeling she'd had upon meeting Odessa, her grandmother, for the very first time? Juniper reached into her pocket and squeezed the blue stone, Odessa's parting gift. *It brought me luck,* her grandmother had said. Maybe it would for Juniper, too.

Someday, when this was all over, they needed to have a big reunion—but with *all* the family this time. It was seriously overdue.

With a sigh, Juniper drew her gaze in from the far mountains and focused back toward home. *Someday.* Meanwhile, closer to hand was the Bazaar field, where the merchants were nearly done setting up for the looming festivities. Where Root was stashed, along with their horses, awaiting the time to meet up. Where Team Bobcat was gathered, no doubt ready with their disguises and refining their plan for palace infiltration. And closer still were the dungeons, where Juniper's own father, and Jess and Egg's father, and Erick's father, and so many other fathers and mothers and sons and daughters lay captive and unreachable.

Awaiting the force that would set them free.

11

"IT'S A BOONDOGGLE, INNIT?" SAID LEENA
that night, the end of their third full day back in the palace, as they
all gathered together to vent their frustrations on a bowl of leftover
cornmeal mush and spiced apples.

Oona nodded. "We're doing all this skulking and gathering,
but to what end? We're no closer now than when we got here, not
really."

"We're in the uphill part," Juniper reassured them. "That horrible, slow gathering climb. But once we reach the peak and get
ourselves together, we're going to get some speed on the down-go
that'll whip your hair straight back, mark my words." The others
smiled a little, and Juniper was glad for this. The mood had been
increasingly gloomy of late. "Now, let's get down to business. What
are our actual goals? What can we do to reach them?"

"We need to hit this head-on and take down the Mantis," said
Jess decisively. "She's the number one bad guy right now. Topple
her, and the castle is ours."

Egg shook her head firmly, and Jess narrowed her eyes.

"I'm with Egg," Leena said. "How can we possibly snare the Mantis? Don't you see all the guards she's got with her every moment of the day?"

"I agree, there's too many unknowns for us to try a direct attack," Juniper said. "And we still have no idea how loyal her staff is. If even a few are firmly on her side, and we have to assume they are, that's too many."

Jess's shoulders slumped.

"Free the prisoners, then! *They're* not loyal to her," said Tippy.

"That's the goal, all right," said Erick.

"But how can we do that?" said Oona, twisting a strand of hair nervously around her finger.

"We can't," said Jess. "Why? Because we can't get into the dungeon."

"Maybe we should be thinking small," said Erick at last. "Looking for little ways to undermine her around the palace. Nibble away at her control, you know?"

"Like a mouse war!" offered Tippy brightly.

"And what good will that do exactly?" challenged Jess.

"Erick is right," said Juniper. "Little pranks and mischiefs won't get us back the castle, but they will get the wheels rolling. Give us something to do while we look for a bigger inroad—or till we can make our own. We'll hack away at a load of small cracks until together finally they form a giant gaping hole."

Leena looked unsure. Oona looked faintly green.

"Look at it this way," said Juniper. "We have four days till the launch of Summerfest, when the Bobcats come in the gates and we can meet up with them. Then the opening festivities kick off and things really start moving. That's when we'll be expected to strike; Cyril will have given his information to the Mantis by then if his father's still out." Picturing the motionless body in that darkened room, Juniper could not imagine Lefarge leaping up to lead a charge against them any time soon. It was painfully obvious he would be down for a while. How long till Cyril came to the same conclusion and confided in his stepmother?

"So we need to strike before then," said Leena slowly.

"That's right," said Jess. "If we don't take back the castle before Summerfest, we've failed."

"I wouldn't go that far," Juniper said. "But certainly by then Cyril will have everyone on high alert. What we really need to do is nail down a concrete plan. I think we should take a few more days to ramp up our spy schedule, then pool it all and see where we're at. Set our course forward. But in the meanwhile"—Juniper grinned wickedly—"let's look for ways to cause as much chaos and confusion as we can."

Erick nodded. "Think of ways to subvert the Mantis's authority. Little things here and there—if we can get her to cast suspicion on everyone around her, get her angry with them, doubting them, questioning their loyalty, so much the better. Confusion, misattribution, you get the idea."

"Bring on the havoc," Tippy chirped gleefully. "Oh, I like the sound of this!"

"You stick with me, chicklet," said Juniper, tucking Tippy under her arm. "There's an art *and* a danger to chaos making, you know."

And so they dove into the guts of the palace, lurking and flitting about, slipping out to tip flowerpots and topple buckets and overturn chairs. They sliced drapes and bumped pans heaped with coal dust. Juniper knew that the immediate blame would fall upon the staff, and this pained her. But it couldn't be helped.

As the visible face of their operation, Egg continued her work in the palace. She snooped on those rooms not easily accessed via the Pockets. She mingled with the guests and nobles—most notably through her archery jousts—and kept an eye on that side of things. She also kept the group supplied with food and drink, though Juniper was not entirely sure where it all came from or how she managed to avoid suspicion. Perhaps Cook thought she was just an exceptionally peckish girl?

Egg hinted at a further solution she was developing: a special key, she said. A way to get them inside the dungeons. But when Juniper pressed her for more information, Egg simply wrote, "Not ready yet." When it *would* be ready—or what "it" even was—was anyone's guess.

And so they carried on.

Tippy, being small of frame and light of foot, took to the Pockets better than any of them, often disappearing for long hours that left Juniper faint with worry. Each time the little girl came back with sad eyes and tight lips, but only shook her head when Juniper asked what was up. This was so unlike Tippy that Juniper was on the point of calling an intervention when, early on their fifth day back in the palace, a small clammy hand shook her awake.

"Shhhh!" Tippy said, pushing her fingers onto Juniper's mouth for extra muffling.

Juniper gagged and swatted away the treacle-sticky hand. "What is it?" she whispered, sitting up.

Along the Aerie floor, Erick, Leena, Egg, and Jess were sprawled out in their bedrolls. Various rugs, pillows, and duvets had been heaped for maximum comfort (Fleeter was tucked and purring under Jess's outstretched arm), but the conditions were still rustic at best. Outside the huge windows, the first crack of dawn was splitting the sky with the promise of a bright day to come.

What on earth could have Tippy up and around so painfully early?

When they had ducked down the steep staircase from the trap-door and settled in the dark hall below the Aerie, Tippy's mouth dropped open and everything poured out in a single breath: "Oh, mistress Juniper, 'tis only my sister Elly I've been a-worried about this whole time. Her being in the dungeon—she's your top maid and fully devoted to Your Royalty, don't I know it, and so completely never would have sworn that foul allegiance oath—so of course she's certain to be locked away there. But how can I know for true she's well? What if she's taken sick or needs something?"

Tippy choked, and Juniper caught a flailing hand in both of hers. "Oh, Tippy! I should have thought of how hard this is—I know how much Elly means to you. But we're working to free the prisoners just as fast as we can."

"I know, but they're trapped down in that dark place, all

of them and my Elly along with, and I just can't bear it." Tippy scrubbed her face with her free hand, but the other tightened in Juniper's. "Not when I might *do* something, don't you know?"

Juniper froze. "Tippy. What have you done?"

"'Tis a good thing. You can trust me, truly." The little girl took a deep breath. "Only here is what I am doing and did and have to do, and you can't stop me, Your Most Royal of Junipers, and sorry I am to have gone behind your back, but I spoke with the house-keeper already, and—and I have gotten myself hired on as a second underscrubber." With that, Tippy fell silent.

"Wait, you—*spoke* to someone? Here in the palace?"

Tippy hung her head. "I needed to, don't you see? They don't know me. I don't know most of them new people here now, and even Cook what was here before—even she don't remember me. I'm a wee fry, aren't I? An' look even smaller than I am. Who would remember little me as anyone in particular?"

"Why, Tippy! Who *wouldn't* remember you?"

Tippy scoffed. "You say that now, Your Stouthearted Royalty, because we're of the Queen's Basin and we traveled together, and also I'm such a sparkling character and all. But out there in the palace? It's not like that. I'm kitten's paws out there."

"What about Cyril, though? He'd know you sure enough."

"That prig? He won't come within sixty snoozes of the kitchen. Anyway, I know how to stay out of sight. Not a person will know me for one of your team, I promise it," Tippy said. "Scrubbing's the worst of jobs; everybody hates it. They jumped at the chance for an extra pair of hands. I'll weasel myself into the palace, find a spare set of keys if they are to be found, get as close to the dungeon as I can. I'll get you all the information there is, Your Majesty, I swear it. I'll get it for you, and for Elly most of all."

Before Juniper could decide what she thought of this, Tippy planted a moist kiss on her cheek. Then the newest palace under-scrubber stood ramrod straight, pinched her thumb and index finger together at the side of her lips, and twisted as though turning a key in a lock.

"Not a word from my lips till I get us what we need," Tippy whispered. She spun theatrically in place, half tripping over her tangled skirts, then ducked behind a baseboard and disappeared from sight.

12

THE REST OF THAT DAY PASSED IN A ROUTINE
that was growing uncomfortably familiar: busy, yet heavy with
the syrupy sense of moving without getting anywhere. Early
afternoon found the group scattered across the Aerie floor like
a passel of limp dishrags. This whole spying/mayhem-making
business was taking more energy than they'd expected. They'd
seen a certain amount of success—tensions were high in all areas
of the palace—but as for how or even *if* it was advancing their
plan, that was a lot less certain.

Brushing self-doubt aside, Juniper turned to Tippy, whose
visible air of spizzerinctum suggested she had news to share.
"Tipster?" she asked.

Clapping in delight at being called on first, Tippy leaped to the
center of the room (carefully avoiding the trapdoor, though it was
shut tight), where she executed an awkward pirouette. When all
eyes were on her, Tippy stopped whirling and gave a deep bow. "My
fellow Goshawks," she said gravely. Then she cracked up, slapping

her knee and sinking to the floor in unbridled laughter. "Never mind all that. Only I've got some premium news, and thought I might take the chance to show off my newest dance move first. Didja like it?"

"What news, you insufferable child?" said Jess.

Tippy shrugged, yawned, and stretched. "Only that I've been in to see the king."

The room erupted. Juniper flew nearly halfway across the room before she got hold of herself. Not for the first time she was very glad of the Aerie's height and isolation from the rest of the palace, as the tumult rose to the (very high) rafters. Finally Juniper waved her hands, stopping just short of her trademark piercing whistle. *That* would bring folks running, no doubt!

"Tippy," she said instead, "be reasonable and stop preening. What do you have to share?"

"'Tis all just a day in the life of an underscrubber," said Tippy airily, wallowing in the attention. Then she grinned and got serious. "All right, I haven't *quite* seen him to his very royal face. Only, I've been looking for a way to jailbreak my sister, Elly, right you know it. So this has taken me to a lot of hanging about the entryway to the dungeons, chatting up the guards and such."

Leena groaned in exasperation. "Have you no sense, you gosling?"

"You said you were to be safely stowed in the kitchen!" said Juniper, aghast.

"My sister is under lock and key!" Tippy exploded. "And a whole wagonload of fathers and mothers and more right along with her. If I'm in a place where I might do something, how could

89

I not? At any rate, most everyone around here has a friend or family member in lockup. It's the most natural thing in the world for me to be gadding there all curious-like."

Juniper didn't know about that, but she nodded for the little girl to continue.

"Anyway, I did it smart-like. The kitchen maids take in big lumpy pots of stew and the like with a heap of pewter plates for the prisoners' suppers. But they also have a separate covered dish what goes careful-carried in the door each mealtime. For their extra-special prisoner, don't you know it? Anyway, with all this stuff, they need extra hands, and sometimes I get myself brought along to help lug the flatware." She shrugged. "Us kitchen gals don't get inside the dungeon doors, the guards take the stuff from us. But it's a reason to hang around. So I did. I just kept on asking the guards about Elly and finally . . ." She fluffed her hair. "Finally the main guard told me to get lost and stop causing trouble, or he'd lock me up with her."

Oona gasped. Juniper felt sick to her stomach.

"Wait, the story's not over! So I went all a-wail, as you know I can do." Oh, Juniper knew! "Then the other guard started yelling at the first, and the third trotted over to yell at the both of them, and what in all the ruckus did I do? I grabbed the key and yanked the handle and bipped myself inside." She waved a hand at the blank faces before her. "Only for an eye's blink, you understand. They're ever so brisk and efficient, those guards. But I got away down the staircase afore they nabbed me. I didn't see which cell Elly was in, for my deepest sadness. But I *did* see the king, just as clear as day. He's stuffed in a big, lighted center cell, all the way down the stairs and far inside the main quadrant. He's just as locked up as you could imagine: bars clear to the roof and surrounded by all the guards in the world." Her shoulders slumped a bit. "But he's there and he's safe. So there you have it. That's my news."

This report slammed into Juniper with such mingled hope and desperation that she felt faintly overwhelmed. So much so that she completely tuned out as the conversation carried on around her with equal parts shock and upset and admiration, all of which Tippy lapped up with pride. Finally Juniper shook herself long enough to wag a finger at the girl. "You can't ever pull another stunt like that, Tipster! Do you know how dangerous that was?"

"I do know," said Tippy. "Them guards were sore as bees on a bottom! I had to bring out all my weeping tears to pacify them, and even that barely worked. I know 'twas foolish, but——" She clenched her jaw, suddenly looking a good deal older than her age. "But if we're not here to do what needs doing, then what is the point of us? I won't take unnecessary risks, Your Very Juniperest, but we're all here to save the day. And sometimes, the day just won't save itself without our giving it a good shove."

This was far too close to Juniper's own train of thought, so she let the subject drop and turned to the news gathered by the rest of the spy team: a heated argument overheard between Cyril and his stepmother, he accusing her of not spending enough time with his father, and she threatening to bar Cyril from the sickroom if he didn't pipe down. Lefarge himself had yet to regain consciousness; he didn't even know his son was back in the palace. *And so much the better,* Juniper thought firmly. Cyril deserved no sympathy right now, even if she knew how it felt to have a father out of reach.

The news reports carried on: There was a big renovation project going on in the Glassroom (a round growing-room with walls made all of glass, which housed the king's most rare and prized flowers; the whole chamber was fixed to a fat stone column and could be slid up or down upon the gardeners' whims). The guests seemed to have all arrived—except the Monsian contingent—but less than half the usual guest suites were filled. Was it happenstance or a deliberate slight to the new impostor queen? And were all these nobles solidly on the Mantis's side if they came to her shindig? Or could some be pure rubberneckers, here to see which way the dross was blowing? Or, worse, gossipmongers looking for the latest in the sordid saga of Torr Castle?

It was anyone's guess, and pondering it made Juniper's head hurt. When the telling finally died down and everyone went quiet and looked to her for what came next, all she could think to say was, "We know where my father is. Tippy's laid eyes on his very spot. That means we need to act. We *need* to get into that dungeon."

"But her report makes it clearer than ever. His Majesty is locked up tight," said Leena.

Erick looked at Egg, who was sitting next to him. He touched her shoulder and pointed to her lap, which was scattered with assorted metallic doodads, then asked, "How is your work going?"

"I am still working," said Egg. Her hands flashed along with her spoken words, and Juniper noticed her fingers looked dull and dusty gray. Her fingernails were chipped and cracked. What on earth could she be doing?

"Oh, do tell us more," said Oona. Then she shifted her body into Egg's line of sight and repeated the words, blushing a bit.

Egg shook her head. "It is going slowly," she said aloud, apparently unwilling to stop her work long enough to write on her armband. "I need more time."

"Time?!" Leena yelped, and Jess cut in, speaking her words as she signed them: "We're running out of time, you know that!"

Egg tilted a stubborn chin at each of them in turn, till she'd come around the circle back to Juniper. "I can do this," she said. "My device will get us into the dungeon. Now let me be until I am ready."

With that, she waved an arm to show the subject was closed, and redoubled the speed of her lap-work. Her gaze, though, stayed focused on the conversations around her.

"Ah, er," said Erick. "Ahem. I have some news of my own as well."

"You do?" said Juniper.

Erick nodded. "I have something to share. I wasn't sure it was of much use—it's a bit of a tangent, you'll see. But now I see there could be, ah, some connection."

"Oh, do stop yammering and get to the point," said Jess.

"Er. So I was in the library earlier today," Erick said, then quickly added, "I was hidden in the Pockets, truly! . . . All right, I *did* venture out into the stacks, but only for a moment." He scooted a pile of books farther behind him. "At any rate, there was a committee meeting being held in a back room: a discussion to do with the entertainment."

"Team Bobcat!" cheered Tippy.

"My thoughts exactly," said Erick. "The group was discussing a list of those who were seeking to perform during Summerfest. They didn't *exactly* say they needed more performers, for they had a fair number. But some of their comments make me think they aren't too happy with some of the quality. They could use better talent. In fact, they're putting out one last open call for new performers, tomorrow afternoon."

Leena looked doubtful. "If it's talent they want, I'm not sure that our Bobcats will——"

But Juniper felt excitement jolt through her. "This could be the very ticket! We'd thought to have Team Bobcat gadding about for the crowds, to provide a distraction *and* escape notice, then creep in the palace some sneaking way. But imagine if they could bring their show *into* the castle grounds! Officially! Only think of the opportunities."

"Precisely," said Erick.

"But the Bobcats don't know about the open call," said Oona.

"They don't know about it *yet*," said Juniper. "It looks like we'll need to plan an excursion to carry out the news."

Oona perked up at this, and Tippy shot a fist into the air. "Yes! 'Tis the night for us to sneak out and party, innit?"

"Most certainly not to party!" said Leena, shocked.

Around them, tantalizing smells were already wafting through the big, wide-open Aerie windows. Tomorrow was Summerfest Eve, and the Bazaar was packed. Every food stall was now set up and fully steaming, sizzling, and sparking for a chance to help hungry fairgoers celebrate.

But Juniper grinned. "Not party as such. But we *have* worked awfully hard. We need to meet up with Team Bobcat and get them that info quick as ever we can. Then we'll nail down the details of our plan along with them and get all our ducks in a row. But"—she shrugged—"once all that's tended to, if we stumble on a nibble of entertainment as we walk? I shan't be one to turn aside."

"Fun and *food*," said Tippy. "What with all our cooking for the palace guests *and* feeding all those prisoners, there's not nearly enough grub to go around in them kitchens."

Juniper froze in place. "What did you just say?"

Tippy gave her an odd look. "Huh? What with the cooking for the palace guests and—"

"Never mind," said Juniper quickly. "Only—you got me thinking about what you said earlier, about the food that goes to the dungeons. That special dish that's carried in every mealtime. That has to be for the king."

"Well, sure. But I don't see—"

"Tippy!" Juniper gasped, jumping up to grasp the little girl by the shoulders. "If I gave you something—a very *small* something— could you slip it into one of the dishes meant for the king? Bury it in the food all sneaky-like, so no one else sees?"

Tippy wrinkled her brow. "Would it, um, be *clean*, this something? If it's going in the king's food . . ."

Juniper grinned. She pulled Odessa's blue stone out of her pocket and turned it so it twinkled in the window's light. "We'll make it clean as can be, you marvelous child. Now, let's get ourselves out into the fresh air, shall we? The Bazaar awaits."

13

IN THE END, BOTH EGG AND JESS DECIDED TO stay back at the palace. Egg was too busy with her solo tinkering mission, and Jess was either helping out or perhaps using her spy skills to raid the Mantis's stash of beauty supplies. And so the haze of late afternoon found Juniper, Erick, Leena, Oona, and Tippy creeping down through the Pockets toward the Great Hall.

"How shall we get out of the castle?" Oona had asked before they left the Aerie. They'd first planned to exit the same way they came in: sneaking through the back cellars, distracting the guard, and so on.

But Leena said, "What's the best way to avoid notice on a day like today?"

Juniper jumped on this. "Hide in plain sight, you're thinking."

Leena nodded. "Summerfest is a madhouse. Tippy here is already part of the kitchen crew, and from all my spying, I think there are so many new helpers and cleaners and pot scrubbers, there's no way for anyone to keep track of who they all are. If we're inside the palace, and we go to leave it, who's likely to stop us?"

"We'll need to keep our heads down, especially knowing that Cyril's a-prowl. But I agree. That should work."

"I can get us back in, too," said Tippy. "They're asking us all to find more helpers for the fest. We can give that excuse to the guards at the gate and come back in just as ever the way we left."

And so the friends made their stealthy way through the Pockets, sliding out one by one to join the army of workers fanning through the palace in a blur of soapsuds and dust brushes and lemon-scented floor polish. In the hubbub, it was easy for them to look busy, then make their quick way out through the wide front gate and down the long road toward the bustle of light and noise that was the Bazaar.

"How can such a place exist?" whispered Oona as they reached the fairgrounds, reunited after their successful escape. They'd seen the clatter and construction going on in the field from the Aerie windows, of course. They'd inhaled countless delicious scents. But being up close like this, *within* it, was another matter entirely. By now the booths were all up and running, every bit of ground jammed with interesting things to see, hear, and smell. And occasionally taste, too, as friendly merchants shared samples of their treats and talked up their work in hopes of luring in more customers.

At one point, Juniper grabbed Erick's arm. "Look over there!" She could have sworn she saw, melting into the crowd just ahead . . . "Cyril," she said under her breath. "Or someone very like him. Did you see?"

Erick said he hadn't, and though they pushed through crowds

and scanned every vendor in sight, Cyril—if he had been there at all—had fully disappeared. As they stood surveying the crowds, a pungent smell caught Juniper's attention. They stood next to a rough-looking stall labeled APOTHECARY BY AGNES. Rough bundles of herbs hung drying from the stall's awning, and a long table was crammed with small pots and jars and stoppered vials. The overpowering odor was herbal and medicinal, but there had been something else—a whiff of something strong and sharp, just for the barest moment, that seemed familiar.

Then it was gone, and an enthusiastic shriek drew Juniper's attention: The rest of the group had come upon Root. As Juniper and Erick caught up with the others, Oona tackled Root in a full bear hug, only to pull back bashfully. (A little late for that, Juniper thought.)

"Hi," Oona said.

"Hi," replied Root.

The others rolled their eyes at the awkward ways of young love, or whatever this was. Then Root shook himself and addressed the rest of the group. "Come on," he said. "I've got the Bobcats, and they'll be very glad to see you."

They followed Root as he navigated them around carts, under low tent awnings, and between hastily assembled booths, until they finally reached a wagon with extra-large mint-green wheels. The body was painted a vibrant purple and emblazoned with huge letters proclaiming THE BALANCING BOBCATS! along with an assortment of poorly sketched felines in various distressing poses.

"This?" said Leena doubtfully.

Juniper studied the image. "Are they meant to be . . . ?" Then she trailed off because, for the life of her, she couldn't imagine *what* they were meant to be doing.

"Balancing, I think," whispered Root. "The creatures are supposed to be bobcats. It's, er, symbolic. Or perhaps ironic?" He shrugged.

Then the wagon door burst open, and there, framed in the cheerful yellow opening and looking every bit her fierce, glorious self, was Alta.

Juniper ran to her friend. It had been too long!

Minutes later, the whole crew had packed inside the wagon, with Alta and the rest of Team Bobcat: Paul, Toby, Roddy, Sussi, and Filbert. Triple bunks were hooked onto each of the walls, and the kids clustered on the lowest of them (the top two were shut, for maximum sitting space). In no time they were tripping over their words in their eagerness to catch up on news and start swapping stories and adventures.

"Balancing Bobcats, eh?" Leena quipped, and titters of laughter followed.

"I did the painting myself," said Sussi with pride.

"It's . . . striking," said Erick.

"To be sure," said Juniper. "Rendered with great, er, passion!"

"As you'd hoped, that costume salesman sold us bunches of his stock for a fine price, and directed us where to get the wagon, to boot," said Alta. "The name of our group just wrote itself." She coughed. "So to speak."

"What sorts of costumes?" asked Leena.

Paul reached under the bunk and yanked out a dramatic armful of brightly colored cloth. "We are all to be creatures, don't you see? Birds and balancing beasts aplenty!"

The room dissolved into general laughter, and Paul grinned along with the rest. Then a thought occurred to Juniper. "What happened to all the horses? I saw only a couple out there with the wagon—we should have a dozen kicking around!"

"Ah, yes," said Toby. "After Root added all your beasts to our own, we knew we couldn't keep the whole pack of them here."

"They stood out like red on white," Filbert confirmed.

"We found someone a ways out willing to stable them for us through the festival. Gave him all the money I had, and promised him more besides when we come back to collect. I, er, hope that's all right?" Toby looked suddenly uncertain.

"Absolutely," said Juniper. "We'll have coin aplenty once we pull off this coup. Whatever gets us there the smoothest is good in my book."

"I saved all the saddlebags and the stuff in them," Root said.

Oona perked up. "Jess asked me about that. She said to make sure I bring back all her salves and ointments."

"They're in the storage compartment below the wagon," Root said, "just outside. If you want to, er, come with me and get them?"

Beaming ecstatically and apparently lost in a world all their own, Root and Oona wafted down the teetering staircase leading outside, while everyone else fought their urge to gag at the syrupy display.

Juniper turned back to the group. "About the balancing," she said. "You're sure you all can pull off the right kind of tricks?"

"We've been practicing," said Roddy. "I've been drawing diagrams and schematics. Now we just need time to get the routine perfect."

"Time I'm not sure we have," said Alta with a sigh. "But never mind that. We just have to play the part, right? No one said we had to be any *good*."

Juniper tilted her head. "Um. Well. About that."

And so the catching-up process kicked off in earnest, one story leading to another and on late into the night, as the transplanted Queen's Basin group pushed in tightly together and planned and plotted, getting ready for when they would join forces to take on Torr Castle.

Slowly, steadily, a plan took shape. They talked it through, looked at it from all angles. It could work. Not a racehorse of a plan, perhaps, but a good solid steed that should get them where they were going.

So. Two days left until Summerfest, and the plan was in place. There were variables, sure. Not least of these were the Bobcats' auditions, and whether Egg would be successful at getting them a way into the dungeon, and the many other moving parts that had to clip into place to make their effort a success.

All that wasn't too much to hope for, was it?

14

WHEN THE CHATTER AND DISCUSSION AND celebration finally wound down, it was late night and well past time for the Goshawks to head for the palace. At some point in the evening, Oona had erupted in a round of spontaneous cartwheeling with her sister Sussi, and ended up electing to stay with Team Bobcat. A bit worried about a big group trying to sneak back into the palace, Juniper suggested that Root and Leena stay out overnight as well, to which both agreed. On the morrow, the two would enter the grounds along with the Bobcats, then slip away once they were inside and use the Pockets to head to the Aerie. That left Erick, Juniper, and Tippy to hug their friends good-bye and get ready to sneak back into the castle.

Juniper had been thinking a lot about whether any of the palace staff might recognize her as the crown princess.

Erick thought not. "There's no way. Not with your—" He waved vaguely at her short, dark hair and her rumpled britches. "Your 'new look.'"

Juniper still wasn't sure, but Leena agreed. "People see what they expect to," she said. "Juniper Torrence will be nowhere near their minds—count on it."

"It's not as though it's the regular castle staff on duty anyway," said Root. He frowned. "Most of the ones who would have truly paid attention are locked away, and more's the pity."

"That's what we're here to fix," said Oona. She put a timid hand next to Root's on the table, so close that the very tips of their fingers were touching. They both went very pink and very silent.

"Ahem," Juniper said. "All right, then. Off we go. I can see that things shall do quite fine back here in our absence."

At the last moment, Juniper swapped a coin for an oversized lollipop from a late-night sweets merchant. With her tousled hair tugged across her face, her boots crusted with mud (her cape had stayed in the Aerie, for better sneaking and lurking), and now a giant sweet jamming up the whole left side of her face, Juniper breezed through the watchpoint without getting a second glance. To Tippy's disappointment, the guards didn't even want to hear her long prepared story about new recruits for the kitchens. They just waved in a bored way and said, "More of the press-gang! In you go, then—join the masses."

Juniper had never been happier for a lazy work ethic in her life—or perhaps *overworked* was a better word for it; after all, these were the same guards they'd seen on the way out, hours and hours earlier.

Leaving Team Bobcat behind had been surprisingly difficult

after being reunited such a short time, but now Juniper's mind—behind the tooth-aching sweetness of the lollipop—was buzzing with the plans they had sketched out together. At last, they had something solid and real to push toward, a concrete way to bring the fight inside the palace.

And they had their top-secret weapon, too. Juniper had taken Paul aside just before they set out and whispered long into his ear. He received the instructions seriously, asked a few questions, then saddled up his horse and galloped off into the night. He would be traveling all the way up the Hourglass Mountains, back into the Anju territory. When they'd last parted, Zetta had assured Juniper that she and her people would support Torr if there was need.

Well, there was need.

Now it remained to be seen whether the Anju would be true to their word. And if so, how long it would take them to gather their forces and reach the palace. After all, the Anju traveled on foot, not by horseback; getting here from their high mountain village could take many days. In truth, the outcome of Paul's long and grueling ride was uncertain at best.

But then, wasn't uncertainty the very name of this venture?

So much bulk often hung upon the thinnest of spines. All Juniper could do was set the body in motion and hope that the rest would follow in due time.

All these thoughts distracted Juniper as they dashed through the dark midnight palace on their way to the nearest Pocket. Then they came around a corner in the west hallway—almost to their entry point, but not quite—and there, just ahead, was Cyril. He hadn't seen them yet; he was frowning down at a thick sheaf of parchment, which held his full attention. But at this late hour, the hallway was otherwise completely empty.

In another moment, he would look up and see them.

It would all be over.

Juniper didn't fear so much for herself; her foppish cousin could scarcely recognize her under this filth and candied sugar, particularly with her short hair and boys' clothing. But Erick and Tippy looked every bit themselves, just as Cyril had known them these last weeks in the Basin. The same outfits, even.

How had they not thought to guard against this?

Just behind her, Tippy froze. Juniper waved a hand. They had to keep moving; an awkward stop would just make Cyril look up sooner. Maybe he wouldn't look up at all?

Cyril let out a weary sigh and rubbed his eyes. She could see it starting to happen as though in slow motion: the rustling of papers, the tightening of his lips, the slow shifting of his gaze.

Acting on impulse, Juniper ran. She tucked her head into her chest and plowed straight for Cyril. His gaze met hers at the last second, but too late: She caught him square in the midsection. Arms windmilling, sheaf of parchment flying, Cyril toppled backward with a winded *Oof!*

Getting the idea, Tippy and Erick ran for the Pocket. Juniper scrambled to her feet, edged behind Cyril, and nudged him back to sitting. His eyes were watery and he was panting for breath.

"Ther', ther', Mister Lefarge, only you were all a-dreamy-like and didn't see me coming for bread or for coin! I'm terribly sorry, I is, couldn't be sorrier. An' I wish I could stay and apologize longer, but alas, I must bolt."

She clapped him awkwardly on the shoulder, then turned and ran, suppressing a pang of guilt. Traitor or not, Cyril had gotten himself a pretty good knockdown.

"Hey, you! Boy!" she heard behind her, in a weak and gargling rasp.

Then she cleared the corner and joined the other two in the safety of the Pockets.

They found Egg and Jess waiting up for them in the Aerie. Egg was still busy with her metal scraps—her fingers grayer and more rusty-looking than ever—now hard at work with several new implements. Her usually tidy braid was askew and her lips flattened in fierce concentration. Jess (perfectly turned out as usual; no dishevelment for her!) had donned a new set of calfskin gloves and was stirring a pot of some cream or other, while Fleeter purred at her feet. Both girls set aside their projects while Juniper and Erick caught them up on recent events, including the near catastrophic run-in with Cyril.

"Too close for comfort," said Erick, his face still shiny with sweat. "*But* I'm happy to say it wasn't for nothing." With a flourish, he whipped a sheet of parchment from his inner vest pocket.

"You got that off Cyril?" said Juniper, impressed.

"Off the floor, technically," said Erick. "His pile went every which way, and I figured it couldn't hurt to know what had him so absorbed." With that, he leaned over to study it, and Juniper scooted near to look as well.

"And?" said Jess. "What is it, then?"

Erick frowned. "It looks like . . . medical charts? This might be body temperature; there are lists of medicines . . ."

Juniper couldn't make heads or tails of it. "It's complicated, all right. But look here—that's dated a week ago."

"Someone who was sick a week ago," said Tippy.

"There was a mighty sheaf of papers in that stack—a complete medical record, looked like."

Erick and Juniper looked at each other. "Rupert Lefarge."

Jess nodded. "Yes. But *why* is Cyril studying his father's medical records so intently in the dead of night? What could he possibly want with them?"

Juniper shook her head. "Well, let's file that away and think about it more tomorrow. It's so late, it's almost gone early again. Still, let's be double careful getting around the palace from here on out. We can't take any risks, not when we're so close."

"So Team Bobcat will be ready for tomorrow?" asked Jess. "Did you see them perform?"

"They *say* they'll be ready," said Erick.

"I bet they're marvelous," said Tippy. "Light as feathers, the lot of them." She got on tiptoes to demonstrate, although the main takeaway ended up being that it was a good thing Tippy was not part of the Balancing Bobcats.

• • •

In the end, the Bobcats and their skills came through spectacularly. By craning rather perilously out one of the Aerie's windows, the more curious Goshawks were able to follow the open-air tryouts. They couldn't see much detail from that height and angle, but the group looked sharp and professional—not to mention exceptionally colorful. (Which might have done the trick on its own, honestly.)

The more Juniper watched how they blended and wove as a group, crouching and toppling and twirling, the more she could tell that the energy she'd sensed when they'd all gathered in the wagon wasn't just about keeping to a plan. They wanted to be good at what they did, sure. But it was more than that: Honestly, they looked like they were having a wagonload of fun.

From the hearty cheers that the group sent up after the organizers gave their decision, it looked like the Balancing Bobcats were officially on the roster of Summerfest entertainers.

Still riding the high wave of the Bobcats' enthusiasm, Juniper and the rest of the Goshawks (including Root and Leena, who had made it safely back up to the Aerie) recounted the new plan to Jess, who relayed it in detail to Egg. The very next day was Summerfest Eve: the day that would officially kick off the festivities. On that evening, the palace always hosted a special gala to celebrate the nobles, dignitaries, and high-placed invitees who were sufficiently in the palace's good graces to get on the exclusive guest list. Based on their spying, the gala was proceeding as planned.

On the morning after that, Summerfest would begin. Bright and early on Day 1, the castle gates would open wide to let in the crowds who had eagerly awaited this event all year long. In honor of his people, King Regis always had the palace and the grounds specially decked out, and this year looked as busy as ever. A giant stage had been set up in front of the decorative fountain in the Small Gardens, which would be used by the approved performers. From her high vantage point, Juniper could see crowds already in line at the gates—a full day in advance!—made up of early birds eager to get first pick at the food and viewing pleasures afforded by Torr Castle.

And here was the first stage of their plan: Dilute. They would wait till as much of the crowd was inside the gate as possible. All those additional bodies would redirect most of the guards to manning the gates and to patrolling and monitoring the gardens and grounds.

"That's when we'll start to make our move," said Juniper.

"And we're really sure about this move?" asked Jess.

Juniper sighed. "It's our only shot right now, and honestly, I think it's a good one. We have to count on the support of the townspeople and villagers. They're citizens of Torr, every one of them. They have no titles or lands or positions to be bought off by the Mantis and her ilk. They love my father, they love me, and many loved my mother more than their own family, for all she did for them."

Thus was the plan's second stage: Divert. The members of Goshawk *and* Bobcat, by then having accessed the castle grounds, would skim through the crowds, exposing Malvinia Lefarge's treachery and her nefarious plans to the common people and telling them to spread the word out farther.

"Don't you see? Everyone is wondering what's become of King Regis. The Mantis is going to put about some sob story, some tragic reason why the king has been 'away' these past weeks. Who knows what bogus tale she'll make up to yank the wool over people's eyes? But whatever it is, all we need to do is get the truth out there. That's it! We'll lay bare her betrayal and her double-dealings. Tell them she's got the real, true king locked up, and that she's stealing the throne out from under him as surely as we're standing right there!" Juniper fought to control herself. "We do this, and they'll be eating out of our hands."

"If you say so," said Jess, looking uncertain.

Finally would come the third phase: Deploy. The newly enlightened crowds would begin making a fuss, heckling and challenging and perhaps even storming the Mantis's throne just a little. Juniper allowed herself the luxury of imagining a little roughing up for the impostor, but the truth was, the false queen would have guards all around her. Which was part of this step, too.

"Even more guards will be drawn away to deal with the ruckus," Juniper summarized, "protecting their charge and maybe starting to herd people out of the castle grounds. Either way, they'll be kept busy. That's when *we* head for the dungeons."

"They won't leave them unguarded," said Erick.

"No," said Juniper, "but you know a rabble-rousing crowd will be seen as a bigger threat than a bunch of locked-up prisoners. They might leave a token watchman, but mark my words, if there's a big enough clatter out of doors, the guards will clear out of that hallway like flies off a clean sheet. Not for long, mind you, but they will go."

"Not only that," said Tippy, "but His Woefully Locked-Up Majesty will be ready for us. Right?" She looked at Juniper, who nodded.

"I've given Tippy the blue stone that was my mother's. She's going to put it in his food tomorrow."

"How exactly is the king to know this mysterious blue stone is a message from you?" asked Jess.

"It was a gift from my grandmother Odessa," said Juniper. "It's clearly not a Torrean stone—I believe it will be distinctive enough to betray its Anju origins. If he doesn't figure out the stone is from me, he will at least know *something* is going on. My father is a smart man. He will be on the alert, and ready to leap to action when the moment arrives."

"We just need to be able to get *into* the dungeon when it does," said Jess, with a pointed look at Egg.

"Right," said Juniper, not needing to look at Egg to know what her answer would be. "So let's talk about keys. What are our options?"

Erick said, "There are only two keys to the main dungeon entrance: one around the waist of the Mantis herself, and the other in the pocket of the chief guard on duty, who unlocks for the changing of guard twice a day."

"What about the individual cells?" Jess asked. "Are those locked separately?"

Erick nodded. "They've each got their own separate keys. I'm guessing there's some big receptacle or board in the main room, so they're all out in the open in full sight."

Juniper nodded. "Easy for the guards to get to *and* for them to keep an eye on."

"So all that's holding us back is the key," said Jess, again putting extra emphasis into the signing portion of her speech.

Juniper said, "She's working as fast as she can. Now we need to do our part: get ready and also look out for other ways to get those keys. That's all the plan we've got so far."

Egg and Jess seemed locked in some private unspoken rivalry. Root and Leena looked game for anything. Tippy was close to falling asleep right there on the carpet, her legs curled close under her mud-streaked gown.

"It could work," said Erick.

"It *will* work," said Juniper. "If we move fast, we can be in and out of the dungeons while the guards are still duking it out with the crowds. *And* now we know my father is in there. So even if all we have time to do is get him out, that will be enough. Once we get the key and set him free, the Mantis's reign is over."

Jess pursed her lips. "Foolproof!" she said sarcastically. She glared at Egg.

Juniper shifted uncomfortably. She knew full well that the plan was hardly foolproof. As plans went, it wasn't great; in fact, it was about as holey as a cheese grater. But for now, it was all they had. And one thing was sure: standing still would take them nowhere at all.

It was forward or bust.

15

THE COMING GALA HAD EVERY WORKER IN the palace humming early the next day, and the buzz only grew as the day went on. The main floor of the palace was a veritable hive of busy bees—including the Throne Room (which had been opened into its larger Grand Ballroom space), the library, and a number of smaller parlors and gathering rooms for guests who wanted to dip in and out of the evening's more noisy entertainment. Bodies were at work everywhere: dusting, sweeping, mopping, polishing, waxing, painting, retouching. The parade was endless. The whole day wrung out of Juniper a deep nostalgia. It was so very much like any other Summerfest Eve; she kept half expecting her father to stride around a bend, inspecting the garlands or running through the guest list one last time.

But this was no regular Summerfest Eve, and her father would come nowhere near the guest list—nor anywhere ever again, if that evil Praying Mantis and her sinister stepson had their way.

"Everyone ready?" Juniper said to her skeleton crew.

They were ready—those who were still here, anyway. Team Bobcat had settled with the other performers into the exercise area behind the stables, and by all accounts, they were practicing their hearts out. Oona had permanently joined the Bobcats. Egg had barely moved from her spot all day, keeping busy on her widgets to the exclusion of all else. She clearly knew how much hung on this promised key. Tippy was at her scrubbing duties and had managed to draft Leena to help in the kitchens with her. Between them, they'd managed to smuggle Odessa's blue stone into the royal meatloaf, which headed down to the dungeons at midday. Now it was just a matter of waiting, though Leena and Tippy were kept so busy at their work that the others scarcely saw them for the rest of the day.

This left Juniper, Erick, Root, and Jess to spy on the evening's gala.

"The Mantis has promised her big announcement tonight," Juniper said, "so we've got to be on peak alert. There's so much we need to know: Who is she paying special attention to? Who is currying her favor? Can we overhear any mutterings of discontent or division? Basically we're looking for anything at all to help us in the next phase of our plan."

"Tomorrow," said Erick, with a tiny shiver.

"Tomorrow," Juniper confirmed. It was both right around the corner and impossibly far away. *Hold on, Papa!* she thought desperately, wishing that her blue stone could have had some encouraging words scratched onto its polished surface. *We're coming to save you!*

· · ·

The four subversives wound through the Pockets to the main floor, where they went their separate ways. The spyholes and viewing nooks were scattered all over the huge ballroom, and they had each staked out a spot to get eyes on a different section of the room. Jess would patrol the smaller adjoining chambers in case any private gatherings merited overhearing. Fleeter was deputized to guard the cushions in the Aerie, since sleeping seemed to be his main superpower.

Juniper herself squeezed into the tiny unused hat closet she had first shown Erick all those weeks ago, before their trip to Queen's Basin. She remembered the two of them peeking out at the festivities—what a different party that one had been! Juniper's thirteenth Nameday celebration, and all she'd had on her mind was settling Erick into his place and then breezing out in her finery, to sit near her father's throne and enjoy the evening.

Juniper hadn't expected this to be an easy night, but she hadn't realized just how tough it would be. She twisted the false hook and lowered her eye to the peephole.

The ballroom was at once achingly familiar and yet wholly different. Guests milled around, sipping at their goblets and munching on delicacies. The tall balcony doors had been thrust open to let in the warm night air, and the orchestra at the far side of the room played a peppy tune.

But all Juniper's attention was on the great golden throne— her father's own seat—which was occupied by none other than

Malvinia Lefarge. No one else was up on the dais with her: not her husband (at last report still unresponsive in his chambers), nor Cyril, nor even the elusive young Artie, who seemed to spend more time out of sight than just about anyone. No, the Mantis sat alone, like a proud lioness surveying her domain. Juniper pushed her hands hard into her sides; punching the walls right now would do nobody any good.

The would-be queen stood. She strode to the center of the dais at the front of the Throne Room. She raised both hands.

Gradually, the crowds quieted. It was time for the proclamation.

Having gained the attention of the crowd, the Mantis took a moment to bask. Her cheeks quivered in delight, and her neck was so heavy with jeweled chains, Juniper thought she might topple right over.

Maybe that was just wishful thinking.

Still, her head was bare—and how that must gall her, Juniper thought, to not yet be wearing the crown of Torr. Tonight was a crucial element of the Mantis's plan: spinning her story that would brush the king out of her way in the people's eyes, freeing her to become the new ruler of Torr.

But what about Rupert Lefarge? Would she wait for her husband to regain his health before the coronation?

Somehow, Juniper didn't think so.

The Mantis opened her mouth wide. She did not devour anything, but her wordspew was bad enough. "Ladies and gentlemen," she oiled. A liveried servant held a gleaming silver cone below her mouth. Her voice echoed around inside the bell and blasted out in all directions. "Guests from near and from far—I am *so* pleased to welcome you to Torr Palace, and to this celebration launching our most pivotal event of the whole year: the grand Summer Festival!"

Can't even get the name of the festival right, Juniper fumed. And her father had never needed props to get his people to hear him!

Juniper scanned the audience. So far, all looked attentive (except one shabbily dressed group, which was steadily working through the snack table). Three scribes sat below the dais, taking down every spoken word, and four runners stood stretching their arms and legs, presumably ready to dash any proclamations far and wide.

But she was losing track of her enemy's speech.

"—this glorious day, which shall launch an era that shall be talked about for generations!" There was a pause while the guards, servants, and throngs of guests applauded politely. The Mantis's face took on a look of ineffable sadness. "Before we go any further— and there is good news ahead, a great deal of it—I must first get the bad news out of the way. All of you have surely noticed the change in the leadership of Torr Castle. King Regis of Torrence has not been seen for weeks, and many are wondering, What has become of him? What will become of Torr?" She brought a hand to her brow. "Friends, here is the truth: Regis Torrence is a traitor and a rogue. He spent his reign stealing money from the royal treasury, living in luxury, and consorting with base elements."

Shock froze Juniper's mind to ice. A murmur rose from the crowd, but the Mantis silenced them with a gesture. "There is more—oh, there is much more!" She sighed deeply. "My people, I hoped to spare you the pain, for I know how you loved him. As did I, oh, so dearly!" Her voice hardened. "But there is no sugarcoating the truth. I know you have seen the desolation extending all the way up the White Highway. How many fields burned? How many have lost their livelihoods? This, my people, *this* is what happens when weakness and corruption hold the throne."

Juniper felt like throwing up. How could the Mantis blame the Monsian raids on her father?

"These are desperate times, my people of Torr. And sometimes the sweetest-looking plant can hold the most foul and rotten root. It is for this reason—the deep love and loyalty I bear to Torr—for *this* reason I have arisen to the throne of Torr. And you, people of Torr, can now rest easy. You are safe from the machinations of this evildoer. Regis Torrence will never be allowed to rule Torr again."

The muttering was growing louder, but Juniper couldn't tell if the noise was anger or shock. The Mantis raised her voice still more. "At the end of this week, I—Malvinia Lefarge—shall be crowned Queen of Torr on this very dais. And you shall all be my witnesses. Until then, there is much to be done, and a ruler cannot be too vigilant. For this reason, we have made several changes from how things were run in years past.

"First: We will not be opening the gates to the public on the morrow. The opening-day gala and feast within the gardens shall proceed as planned, but for a preapproved list of high-ranking guests only—including you in this room, of course. Beyond this, a small rotation of common folk may be allowed to filter through. But only such as can be easily contained, and only for short periods."

This brought the barest muttering from the crowd; only commoners, after all, were being kept from the castle grounds.

But Juniper's mind went into a further tailspin. Not only had they lost the element of surprise—how could they reveal the Mantis's plans, after all, if those plans were already out in the open?—but now they had lost their crowds, too. What were they going to do? Pushing down her panic, she listened for what else the woman might dredge up.

"For my next proclamation: We shall see the arrival of some important dignitaries several days hence—representatives from the nation of Monsia. I know that as Torreans, our relationship with our sister nation has been . . . *fraught* at times." *Sister nation?!* Juniper's urge to punch something was now nearly overwhelming. But the speech just wouldn't end. "However, Monsia has been a crucial supporter of your new government, and as such I am proud to declare a brand-new alliance between our two nations. In four days' time, we shall be pleased to officially receive the first delegation from that praiseworthy nation. The Monsians shall be here as our guests, and I trust that this will be the start of a fruitful and long-lasting partnership.

"These dignitaries shall also assist with one very sensitive matter. For the crimes mentioned above, and still more that are not yet made public, Regis Torrence shall be tried and sentenced. And in the interest of fairness—for we wish to display our magnanimity and goodwill—the trial shall not take place here in Torr Castle. Nor shall I myself, as the throne's successor, have anything to do with this judging. Instead, the prisoner shall return at the end of this week to Monsia, where the proper deliberations may unfold in an equitable fashion."

Juniper thought her head was going to explode. How could the Mantis say all those things with a straight face? How could she use the burning of Torrean land on one hand to justify her rise to power, while at the same time presenting Monsia as a cozy new ally? It made no sense. How could everyone listen quietly and go along with it? How could they stand it?

Or maybe they just knew better than to speak out. If King Regis of Torr himself had not been safe from this ruthless impostor, who was?

"There is more good news to share, people of Torr!" Malvinia's voice was choked and slightly breathless. "As you know, the transition of power from one ruler to another seldom runs as smoothly as it might. Our palace dungeons are now filled with those who disputed the change as it was taking place. But to those of you who have family and friends in confinement . . . take heart! For this will be my gift to you, my first edict as your new ruler: Upon the event of my coronation, upon Regis Torrence's exit from this castle, every dissenter shall be released. Yes, I said it! Every last prisoner shall receive a full pardon. Oh, they will need to pledge loyalty to the new throne. But how will they help doing so, being thus pardoned by their rightfully crowned ruler?

"This . . . " She cast her gaze to the ceiling. "This is the love and devotion which I bring to my heavy task as your new ruler. Thank you." She paused again, then bared her teeth in something probably meant to be a smile. "I shall now leave you with one final gift. And reminder."

With that, the Mantis turned and stalked down from the dais. The crowd shifted in place, each person turning to the next as though trying to figure out her final words. Then a visible wave swept through the crowd: hands grabbing arms, jaws dropping, shoulders trembling, and a body or two swooning in place.

Juniper craned to see where they were all looking, but while her spyhole gave her a fair view of the ballroom, its range was limited. Whatever had transfixed the crowds was completely out of her sight.

She had to see what was happening.

With a slam, the door to her spy closet was flung open. In the doorway stood Erick, his face chalky. "Don't look," he stammered.

"Don't look at what? I can't see from here—what are they all staring at?" Juniper kept her voice low, but felt panic rising inside her.

Erick shook his head. "Don't worry about it for right now. Let's just get back to the Aerie and then—"

Juniper cleared the two steps between them and grabbed her friend by the shoulders. "Erick," she said, "I'm not some delicate blossom. This is my father's palace, and that usurper is trying to take it over. I *know* how bad and horrible she is. But I *will* know what she is up to!"

Erick slumped. He let out a long breath. "Come on, then," he said. "There's a place we can see from just down the hall." They exited the coatroom and slipped down the hallway. They needn't have worried about being spotted: The halls were eerily bare, not a soul in sight. They ducked into an empty stateroom, and Erick grabbed for the heavy drapes. Juniper just leaped underneath and plastered herself to the plate-glass window.

"It's—it's the Glassroom?" said Juniper, disbelieving.

It was.

King Regis's specially crafted glass planting chamber was being slowly hauled up its tall pillar, whose top reached the upper level of the palace. Juniper remembered that renovations had recently been made to the Glassroom.

What did they do to it?

All the way around the glass dome's peak, a well of lamp oil was kept burning day and night—for the warmth of the plants inside and so watchers near and far could see their lighted beauty. On a moonless night like tonight, the raised Glassroom was a sort of beacon in the night sky.

But what that beacon displayed now was not just lush green leaves and a colorful riot of bright blue, red, and yellow flowers. Suddenly, Juniper knew what the construction had been about. As the glass bubble rose, flaming against the sky, Juniper could clearly see inside it the figure of a man—slightly stooped, rumpled, rather the worse for wear. Very clearly a prisoner and now being made a spectacle.

Locked in the Glassroom was King Regis Torrence.

The Countdown Has Begun

Days until Summerfest begins . . .   0

Days until Team Bobcat's big performance . . .   3

Days until the Monsian reinforcements arrive . . . 4

Days until King Regis is moved to Monsia
and out of reach . . .   7

Days until serious answers and action
are required . . .   MUST HAVE NOW!!!

16

"THIS CHANGES EVERYTHING," JUNIPER SAID the next day, when they were all gathered together back in the Aerie. The Mantis's horrifying revelation had neatly squelched any further spywork the night before, and now the group drooped around the Aerie like a still-life exhibit on Despair. This morning was the official start of Summerfest, and the castle grounds had all the joy of an open grave. Juniper herself was still half in shock from the night before, but all she could think of was to get busy doing something.

Just about anything would do.

"Come on," she urged, "gather round, everyone. Our plan needs some changing, that's true. Fine, a *lot* of changing. Pretty much starting from scratch. But that doesn't mean we won't come up with something just as good in the end. In fact"—she swallowed—"I bet we can come up with an even better one if we try."

"You think?" Jess deadpanned. But she gathered with the others and dropped down on a cushion near the low table. Even Fleeter nosed over, looking for attention after spending so much time alone over the past days. For a wonder, the creature was actually awake!

Juniper had cleared all the food off the table and now set out a sheaf of parchment and her freshly sharpened stylus. Erick's master information list was nearby, too, but Juniper's nerves were badly rattled. She hoped a good list-making session would restore her equilibrium. "Let's start by writing it all out—our tasks and our obstacles."

"We need to find a way to free the king," said Erick staunchly. "That's its own task now, separate from the dungeons."

Juniper wrote that down. "Obstacles?"

"Twenty-four-hour-a-day guard at the base of the Glassroom's pillar," Jess rattled off. "Fully lighted interior, the lamp oil replenished daily, so no sneaking up in the dark. They'll lower the globe once or twice daily, for supplies and waste and so on, but there's a dozen guards posted already, and I'm sure they'll call in more for the occasion."

"How do you get out of that thing?" asked Root.

"There's a metal ladder for climbing up and down," said Jess, "but that's no use to us. Any climbers would be visible to all by day, and the lamplight makes it even brighter by night. No, His Majesty is clean out of reach, and that's a fact."

Juniper recorded all this with a simple nod. None of it was new information, and all of it made her tremble with impotent rage. But the act of writing was already helping her feel more in control. To clearly see and understand the enemy, after all, gives a much better shot at victory.

Or that was the hope, anyway.

"All right, so freeing the king can't be our first task anymore," Juniper said, dying a little as she spoke the words, but knowing they were true. "There's just no way to accomplish it right now. What about the blue stone?"

"Made it through," said Leena. "We got the dishes back empty as usual. Unless something went astray down them dungeon stairs, His Majesty got the message before he was moved."

"For all the good it does him now," muttered Jess.

"So what is our next goal?" Juniper asked.

"Free the prisoners," said Egg aloud. "No change there." She frowned down at her hands, evidently too busy with her work to stop and elaborate.

Juniper sent a querying glance, and Egg's frown deepened.

"Yes," said Erick. "We need to rescue our parents and the other captives. But more than that, think of all the imprisoned guards! If we can just free them, we could get back the rest of the plan."

"But how?" asked Jess.

"The Mantis nixed the crowds," said Juniper. "And put out that horrible story about my father. We've lost the element of surprise, and somehow I don't think we'd be able to rile up the nobles and dignitaries milling around tomorrow. Even if there were enough of them to cause a tumult, which isn't likely. So where does that leave us?"

"We got Tippy's quick-eye view of the dungeon from her look inside," said Erick. "But there's still so much about them we don't know."

Root cleared his throat awkwardly. "I know something of the dungeons. I, er, used to sneak down there a lot back in the day."

Juniper looked up in surprise. Nobles had been given a fair amount of leeway in the lower levels of the palace, and exploring a dungeon that had been empty for decades (during King Regis's reign, that is; now it was full to bursting) couldn't have been any kind of security risk. But it was an odd pastime for a noble. Root shifted. "My life was always so . . . sanitary," he said lamely, "so organized and scripted. Sometimes I just felt like I needed to—see the other side, as it were. Look under the fabric to get at the seams. You know?"

As a matter of fact, Juniper did know. A very similar set of feelings had led her to start her expedition to Queen's Basin.

"Go on, then," said Leena. "Tell us about the dungeon."

According to Root, the dungeon was located directly under the army barracks, accessible through a winding stair that came up directly into the barracks courtyard. At the bottom of the staircase was a small area with a half dozen guards' rooms. That connected to the dungeon proper: a long circular hallway around a wide-open area (until recently housing the king's cell), with individual cells leading off the central room so the guards could keep an eye on all the doors with a minimal patrol area.

"How many prisoners do we suppose are down there?" Erick asked.

"Several hundred at least," said Root. "I've been spying on the guards since I got back in here. As far as I can see, almost no one is allowed near the barracks or the dungeon. Just the guards assigned there. They keep it bare-bones." He seemed put out by this, and Tippy nodded her own sorrowful agreement.

"The fewer guards in the rotation, the fewer there will be for us to contend with," Juniper said thoughtfully.

"That's true. The thing is, though, there aren't *that* many cells down there. With so many prisoners, they're bound to have put some of the overflow, the less high-risk ones, for example, in those outer cells that used to be prison guards' lodgings."

"The ones at the base of the stairs, before the main prison loop?" said Jess.

"Right."

Juniper was keeping up with all this on her parchment sheet. "Let's talk about getting in. If we took care of the guards, how would that work?"

Tippy perked up. "I can help here, from my very own eagle eyes! Here's what I saw in my watching: There's only two chief guard guys what do the overseeing. They trade off one and then another. It's always one of them or the other to unlock the big old dungeon door."

"So the master key never leaves the dungeon, I'm guessing," said Juniper.

"Probably not," said Root. "They would have the new chief guard—the one just starting his duty that day—do the unlocking, when his partner clocks out. Every aspect of the rotation is strict and regimented, from all I've been able to see."

"Me too," agreed Tippy importantly.

"The Mantis sure isn't making it easy," said Jess.

"All right," Juniper said, trying to tamp down her growing frustration. "So we still have the same three goals: Free my father. Free the guards. And, of course, depose the Mantis. The first we can't start with. And the other two . . ."

"It's like a big Gordian knot, isn't it?" said Erick. "All tangled up together. To free the king, we need the prisoners. To free the prisoners, we need the keys. To get the keys, we need to drop the Mantis, but we can't do that without the king. It's like a dog endlessly chasing its tail."

"Not endlessly," said Juniper, throwing down her stylus and jumping to her feet. "There's a solution here somewhere. We've just got to find it." Her head felt full to bursting. Striding to the window, she put both hands on the sill and looked out. The gates wouldn't open to the small groups of commoners until the afternoon, and the miserably empty grounds—on this, the first day of Summerfest, which should be the happiest time of the year!—made Juniper want to cry.

Then something way down below caught her eye. Someone. Juniper narrowed her gaze. Could that be who she thought it was? A bunch of separate elements swirled in her mind: a fallen parchment sheet, a pungent smell, a certain stall at the fair.

Behind her, she heard a shifting in place, then a faint metal tinkling. Then Egg's words, spoken out loud. "Wait. I have something to share."

Juniper was still caught up in the view below, following her quarry with her eyes until she was sure. Then, all at once, everything coalesced into one shimmering point. *Yes.*

Just like that, they were back in business.

Juniper spun around, heart pounding. Egg was signing, her face tense with determination—and something else. Shame? Uncertainty? Juniper listened for Jess's interpretation but kept her eyes on Egg as the story began: "I have been making a key for the dungeons. I wanted to do this alone. It is . . . the way I always work. But the stakes are so high. I am not moving fast enough." She swallowed, looked around the circle, then met Juniper's gaze straight-on with a shy smile. "Maybe this spy no longer works best alone. Maybe I should consider allies. Teamwork."

As Juniper processed this, Egg brought up her tightly closed fist with an air of dramatic reveal. Slowly she turned it over, splaying her fingers wide. Sitting in her palm was a small, spindly piece of metal.

A gnut.

17

AFTER EGG'S REVELATION, THE ROOM ERUPTED in questions and unbridled enthusiasm.

"Let the girl talk," Jess barked. "Just because she can't hear you isn't a reason to drown her out. Clear back to your circle and talk one at a time so she can follow along. Egg's got more to say about the blasted gnuts."

"What *is* a gnut, anyway?" Root asked.

Egg pulled a bag out of the pocket of her split skirts and popped the small metal instrument back into it. "My father's legacy. His invention and his fortune." She nodded to Jess, who continued with a weary eye-roll.

"Our father sells his gnuts up and down the continent. It's a multiuse, multipurpose gadget—an 'anything thing,' he calls it. You can use it to connect stuff, fix stuff. It's endlessly adaptable and absolutely indispensable. According to him." Egg shrugged. "It gets him places, and everyone seems to want five or six of their own. It's given him the money and the excuse to do all his spying. So I guess it really is the magic tool."

"What does that have to do with our key?" Juniper asked.

"The gnut *is* the key," Egg continued through Jess. "It can be made into a device to pick the lock. I am almost there. I just . . . am missing something."

"It's a good plan," said Juniper slowly. The gnut looked all sorts of clever, but to make it into a genuine lock pick? On such short notice? Tinkering time was a luxury they didn't have. Then she thought of what Egg had said. "Teamwork," Juniper mused. She pulled out a sheet of blank parchment. "Egg, can you sketch out what you've got done so far?"

While she did, the others gathered in close to follow.

"This part here," said Root, pointing, "what if you turned it the other way around? The locks in the dungeon are narrow but get wider inside. Once you're through the keyhole, there will be room for the device to ease apart."

Jess huffed. "You need lubricant to make it bend right. I've got a cream that will probably work."

"Erick," said Juniper, "what about that book you were reading the other day? Wasn't there a whole section on metal crafting and mechanical arts?"

Erick reached behind him to scan through a stack of well-thumbed volumes. He eased out the third from the top and began riffling the pages, till his eyes lit up and he swung it open to a page riddled with diagrams and jargon so technical that Juniper saw stars.

Erick set the book down and touched Egg on the shoulder to get her attention. "Can I see what you've got?" he asked.

Egg handed him the bag and Erick poured the gnuts out onto the floor. His fingers started twitching, and his eyes got that glaze that Juniper was used to seeing when Oona looked at Root. Egg met his gaze and grinned.

"I suppose we should give our engineers a little space," Juniper said, keeping her voice low and light. She paused, then made up her mind. "And while they're occupied, I've got an attack-team mission of our own to undertake. A little something I saw out the window is calling our names. Leena and Tippy, you probably need to get back to the kitchens. So Jess, Root—shall we?"

Sneaking out of the castle took more forethought than their last venture, but time was of the essence and Juniper grabbed at the first thing that came to mind. Exiting the Pockets in the deserted pantry, she grabbed two giant burlap bags. One was empty and the other was half full of bread; both were emblazoned with the words MAVENHAM BREADS AND SUNDRIES.

"The palace always needs more bread," Juniper said. "Don't they know there's a party coming up? We should go pay a visit to the baker."

Jess frowned. "But the Mavenhams always drop the bread off themselves."

Juniper winked. "What do you bet the front-gate guards won't know that? Anyway." She looked from side to side in an exaggerated way. "I hear the oldest Mavenham girl, that one who was tired of baking bread all day, she ran off and joined that rogue *former* princess, can you only imagine?!"

Root stifled a burst of laughter, and even Jess quirked her lips. Then, hauling the bags in front of them in a self-important way— drawing as much attention as possible to what they carried and away from the carriers—the three breezed down the hallways, past the wide front doors, through the gardens, and out into the Bazaar.

Juniper had kept her walk stately, if still brisk, as they moved through the palace. Once they cleared the guards, she tossed her bag to Jess and broke into a run.

"Wait," said Jess, grabbing her arm. "Aren't you going to tell us what we're doing?"

This was the part Juniper had been dreading. She knew exactly how her wild-goose chase would sound. But Jess was right; she needed to tell them. "All right—but we have to keep walking. I don't know how long we have. So, I was looking out the window just a bit ago, and I saw a familiar form sneaking through the castle gates: our old friend Cyril."

"Cyril?" said Jess, at the same time as Root said, "Sneaking?"

"Yes to both," said Juniper. She picked up her pace. "When we came out to the Bazaar the other day, I thought I saw Cyril in the crowds. I followed him for a bit but then I lost him near a certain stall. I thought I must have imagined him."

"And now you've seen him again—but how is that important?" said Jess. "Aren't we trying to stay *away* from him?"

"I've been putting some puzzle pieces together in my head,"

said Juniper. "And I'm starting to think that those tiny bits all together make up a big picture that's quite different from what we'd thought."

Root's face did *confused*, and Jess's did *skeptical*.

Juniper warmed to her tale. "Think about it—we're a day into Summerfest, and Cyril has not yet given us away. You know we'd have heard about it if he had! In all our spying, we've never once seen him have a friendly exchange with his stepmother. Not one! Now, it could be that he was loyal to his father, but I find it hard to believe he's in full support of the Mantis's awful ways." She couldn't say that she trusted Cyril, exactly—it was far too early for that. But the more time passed, the more the conviction was growing in her that there might be another side to his story. And she was curiously curious to hear what it was.

The other two digested this in silence.

Then Root said, "Summerfest *has* officially begun. It's not like Cyril isn't expecting us to be here already."

"Exactly!" Juniper replied. "He knows we're going to be here, so what's the harm in accosting him?"

As they walked on, Juniper examined her new plan and its many possibilities. All she'd told the others was true. On the other hand, she wasn't born yesterday. Her gut might lean toward trusting Cyril, but by the goshawk, the rest of her was going to wait till his loyalties were confirmed before acting.

• • •

After that, they shifted into speed mode, zipping around stalls and through knots of people. The usual giddy lightness of Summerfest was cut through with a tangible sense of disappointment. Huge crowds were camped out around the castle, awaiting the opening of the gates to let in the trickle of allotted visitors to view the grounds and the performers. Keeping that out of her mind for now (one problem at a time), Juniper retraced—with some difficulty—the route along which she'd tracked Cyril several days before. Her heart pounded in her chest. How long since she'd spotted him from the window, slinking out of the gates? How long would he be here for?

Then she came around a flower merchant's cart and saw the faded sign reading APOTHECARY BY AGNES. In front of the stall stood Cyril; his shoulders were hunched, as though to draw the eye as little as possible, but it was unmistakably him. He'd shaved off that infernally pretentious barely-there mustache, Juniper noted with satisfaction, so that was one less cause for annoyance. He was speaking with the fresh-faced girl who stood behind the table. She took his coins and pressed a small jar into his hand. Cyril slid that into his pocket with a furtive look over each shoulder, as though afraid of being seen. He didn't look directly behind him, which was just as well, since his three stalkers were right in the open.

Juniper tugged Root and Jess back behind the flower merchant.

"How are we supposed to catch him?" asked Root doubtfully.

Juniper hesitated. She was a talking sort of girl, a lay-it-all-out-and-see-where-we-stand sort of girl, a girl who liked to hit a problem head-on and deal with it right up front. But this was not an everyday scenario. There was too much at stake to risk it all on a slapdash whim.

"I've got this one," said Jess. She reached into her satchel and pulled out a thick yellow handkerchief. "You two get Cyril into that alley over there, and I'll do the rest."

"Wait—what do you have in mind?" Juniper began.

But Root grabbed her arm. "He's leaving!"

"Come on, then," said Juniper. Turning to Jess, with a frown for the yellow cloth, Juniper said, "Don't do anything rash. I want to talk to him first. We'll get him to the alley and see where things stand." Then she and Root strode quickly after the retreating Cyril.

"Here goes," muttered Juniper. Then she called out, "Cyril Lefarge—could that really be you?"

At the sound of his name, Cyril spun in place. He took in the sight of her and Root. His jaw went slack, and his face blanched. "R-Roo—Juniper. It's—you—but—what—why are you wearing—" He shook his head and pulled himself together. "Look, I can't stay and chat right now. I've got to get back to the palace."

"Hey, it's all right—we're in a hurry, too," said Juniper. "We just wanted to talk real quick. Could you give us a second?"

Cyril hesitated, then finally gave a quick nod. Root led the way to the alley Jess had pointed out. They ducked in the narrow, darkened space between a funnel cake vendor and some booth inexplicably shaped like a giant top hat. Jess was waiting there with her arms folded and a calculating look in her eye.

"Look," said Cyril, the second they were in the shadows. "You know I'm tickled pink to see you, but it's really not a good time."

"Bother the time," said Juniper. "There's bigger geese on the wing, and you know it. Now *what* in the name of everything is going on between you and your father and your crown-stealing stepmother?"

Cyril opened his mouth, then shut it again. He shook his head. "I just don't have a lot to say right now."

"Oh, Cyril," said Jess suddenly, "it *is* good to see you!"

She leaped forward and flung her arms around his neck. Puzzled, Juniper noticed that she had unfurled the yellow handkerchief and now held it in her left hand. She clung to Cyril a moment or two. Odd, Juniper thought; Jess had never struck her as the affectionate type. Then Jess stepped back, a pleased half smile on her face. Folding the edges of her cloth inward with exceptional care, she crammed the bundle into a small pouch and stuffed it into her satchel.

"What's going on, Jess?" said Juniper slowly.

"I . . . " said Cyril. He brought a hand to his forehead, pulled it back again. Juniper could see beads of sweat dotting his brow. He swayed, then toppled like an axe-felled tree. Root jumped forward and caught him before he hit the ground.

"What have you done?" Juniper shrieked at Jess.

"Nothing of consequence," said Jess smugly. "Only what needed doing. That was scarlet valerian root tincture, for your information. A potion favored by my father when he needs out of a tight spot. Direct exposure to the skin causes the victim to fall into a dazed sleep almost immediately. As you saw."

"You had no right to just do that all on your own," said Juniper through gritted teeth. "I said to wait."

"I got us our boy, didn't I?" Jess shrugged. "Now we can lug him back to the palace, with no one the wiser and none of his gotta-go-be-oh-so-busy retorts. We'll have him to ourselves in the Aerie to question at our leisure."

Juniper sighed. There was so much wrong with this scenario, she couldn't even begin to break it down. But here they were, and here was Cyril, out cold and breathing in a frighteningly shallow manner. They couldn't just leave him.

"We've even got the perfect means of transport," said Jess.

She tossed the giant MAVENHAM BREADS AND SUNDRIES bag at Juniper's feet like a challenge.

18

THE RETURN TRIP WAS COMICALLY AWKWARD,
but went off without a hitch. Puffing and panting, the three depos-
ited their lightly breathing bread bag in the center of the Aerie.
Despite the late hour, Egg and Erick were surrounded by heaps of
metal bits and bobs. Leena and Tippy had somehow escaped their
kitchen duty and stood watching with rapt attention.

Root wrestled Cyril out of the mouth of the sack while Jess
stood supervising, hands on her hips. Panting with effort, Root
propped the still-comatose Cyril against the side of the couch.

"What's Cyril doing, taking a nap on our floor?" asked Tippy,
incensed.

"Root Bartley," Jess yelped as Root started to walk away, "you
tie that miscreant up at once! Don't give him a chance to escape
now that we've got him good."

Root looked doubtful. So Jess grabbed a thick round of rope
and marched over, as if determined to make sure the job was done

right. She even reached into Cyril's shirt pocket and pulled out a crisp green bandana, which she tied around his mouth as a make-shift gag.

"There," said Jess with satisfaction. "None of that loosey-goosey stuff! Let's see Mister Traitor-Twice-Over try and break out of these bonds."

"Jess," said Juniper, "we haven't even talked to him yet—"

Then Erick let out a sudden crow of triumph and Egg slapped her palm hard on the floor. The look on both their faces—disheveled and weary though they were—was pure exhilaration.

Juniper crowded in close, all thoughts of Cyril blown from her mind. "What do you have? Did it work?"

Egg motioned to Erick to explain. Her eyes stayed sharply on his lips, and Erick kept his body angled toward her as she held up a prickly, spindly-looking device. "Egg had this figured out, all right," he said. "It was pretty much there already."

"Teamwork," said Egg. "All of us did it together." She showed the narrow end to Root and swung the smooth hinge, which smelled of roses, in Jess's direction.

Tippy edged over and poked the metal contraption with a finger.

"This here is the gnut," Erick said, indicating the swiveling joist. "It brings these other metal bits together."

"But what does it do?" Leena asked.

"Do?" said Egg, standing up and signing with extra care. Then she grinned so wide, they could see all her teeth as Jess delivered her message. "This magnificent beauty is a key that will open any lock it meets. An Everykey."

"That's right," said Erick. "We're ready to hit the dungeons."

With the Everykey in hand, the group decided to act that very night. The attack team was quickly decided on: Juniper in the lead, Egg to work the key, and Root as lookout. Jess insisted on coming along as a backup and helper. Erick looked relieved to stay put, and started listing all the important things he would do back in the Aerie—not the least of which was keeping an eye on Cyril. (Though Juniper noticed how his eye kept drifting to a half-open volume with cross sections of jungle plants that was splayed across the table.) Tippy, too, seemed distracted. She held Fleeter in her lap, mournfully feeding him a pasty mush from her outstretched hand.

"If only we'd had this device sooner, before the king was moved," Leena said. "Then we might have freed him and let him take over from there."

Juniper sighed. "That would be too easy, wouldn't it?" The idea of having her father take over the whole battle set off a wistful ache in her heart, followed by the sort of cramp you get when you're gripping the reins of a particularly headstrong stallion and it's all you can do to keep him from barreling away and throwing you headlong to your death. Feelings she couldn't afford right now, even for a moment. She made her voice crisp and business-like. "We've got this, team. There's no time for a long pep talk, much as you know I'd love to give one."

There were scattered smiles around the circle.

"So here's the plan: The four of us will make our way to the dungeon. Root, you'll be in charge of distracting the guard. Then you'll post behind the tapestry at the top of the stairs as our lookout. The rest of us head on in."

By midnight, the dungeon's main entrance had scaled down to one guard. With the use of their Everykey, they would just need to divert the guard's attention for a few minutes to get inside, with the door shut and locked again and no one the wiser. Down the stairs from the main door was the small dormer area, where the overflow prisoners were housed. These were likely to be nobles and other well-regarded prisoners who didn't require the tightest security measures.

"They will be easiest to free," said Jess, striding over to Tippy and holding out her arms for her cat, while Tippy studiously ignored her, "because they're just inside the main door and up the hallway from the prison area proper. We should see to them first."

"They're also less useful," said Erick. "If we can free the palace guards, they will help us fight to free the others."

But Juniper agreed with Jess. "It's too dangerous. Every step we take inside the cells increases our risk. There's a lot more guards on duty farther in, so the quicker we can get willing bodies on our side, the better."

"Aren't you going any farther in, then?" asked Leena.

"Absolutely we are. But it makes sense to start from the outside, get some numbers on our side, then move in deeper as a group.

We may not have soldiers, but there will be enough to form a good ruckus while we free the rest."

"Plus, Father is bound to be in the outer cells," said Jess. "He will be able to direct us. He's a master of strategy." She scooped Fleeter off Tippy's lap and swung him into his customary spot over her shoulders.

Juniper did a double take. "Wait. You're not bringing that cat with us."

Jess looked offended. "This is no mere cat! This is my partner in spying. I wouldn't dream of leaving him back."

"You left him here when we went out to trap Cyril."

"That was different—this is a proper mission, not some jaunt." She sniffed. "Has Fleeter ever been a speck of trouble before? You know he hasn't. And he's saved your royal hide at least once already, so I don't see there's any argument to be made."

Juniper turned to the others for support, but Root just shrugged, and Egg was looking in the other direction. On purpose or by chance, Juniper couldn't tell. Well, it wasn't worth fighting over. It wasn't as if the cat was noisy, and Jess didn't seem held back by him in any way.

"All right, then, it's on your head." As Juniper turned to the door, she caught Tippy staring at her.

Without the cat to distract her, Tippy seemed suddenly awash in emotion. "Oh, Mistress Juniper of the Lock and Key, you *will* look out for my Elly, won't you?" Tippy's voice trembled, and Juniper had an idea of how much it was costing the little girl not to throw herself to her knees and beg to come along on the expedition. Since the fiasco in the Pockets, Tippy had been making a visible effort to control her impulses. Juniper loved her for it.

"Elly will be at the very front of my mind," Juniper promised.

"We'll take care of things back here," Erick said. "You will all be safe, won't you?"

Jess tugged her cloak up under Fleeter's paws and tied it in a smart knot. "Come on, laggards. It's past midnight, and we've got prisoners to free."

While Root produced an alarming clang farther up in the Pockets, the three interlopers slunk out to the brightly lit dungeon entrance and deployed the Everykey. Juniper held her breath while Egg poked and tweaked, her tongue sticking out the side of her mouth and her brows pulled tight in concentration.

This was it. If this didn't work, it was all——

Click.

The dungeon door swung open with a smooth purr. Not a moment too soon, for as they shot through the door and Juniper eased it shut behind them, she could hear the harsh clap of boot heels echoing back down the hallway toward their customary lookout spot.

Juniper, Egg, and Jess ghosted down the twisting dungeon stairs, keeping as light on their toes as possible. They needn't have worried, though. Far from the dank, echoing chamber Juniper had expected, the passageway buzzed and burbled and hummed as though all the sewage and heating pipes of the whole palace might be squashed into the walls above them.

Still, they kept alert and silent as they moved through the eerie, half-lit passage. Jess pulled ahead when they reached the base of the stairs. She quickly bypassed the first three doors, peering inside the small windows until she stopped at the fourth. She signaled Egg to come with the key.

Juniper frowned. Why not start at the beginning? She looked in the door closest to her and saw the slumbering form of Baroness Santopolo, a distinguished noble who had brought a younger Juniper toasted caramels every time she visited, a specialty from her hometown of Wily Narrows in the far north of Torr. But Egg was already moving toward Jess, a spring in her steps that told Juniper who was behind that fourth door.

Pursing her lips, Juniper caught up with them. If it were her father behind one of these doors, wouldn't she rush to get to him first? Of course she would. In truth, they could do worse than having a professional spy on their side. The idea of having an adult around who could take charge and organize things was appealing. Although some part of her—the part that had been crowned ruler of Queen's Basin, that had fought the Anju Trials and survived a boiling flash flood and masterminded their entry back into the palace and was even now formulating plans for its takeover—*that* part did feel just the tiniest bit let down at the prospect.

Still, it was the right thing to do.

Moments later, the lock gave a silky click and the door swung open. Jess was inside before it finished swinging. Egg looked after her into the cell, and Juniper saw the longing in her eyes. Then Egg met Juniper's gaze and waved her lock pick toward the corridor, slipped away, and went to attack their next obstacle.

Juniper followed Jess inside. Rogett Ceward sat up on his narrow cot bed, the sleepy look falling off his face. Jess crouched over him—not hugging but whispering fervently in his ear. Juniper softened. Jess hadn't seen her father in over a month; she must have been worried sick for his safety. But the man looked to be well fed and in decent health.

Rogett squeezed Jess's hand. "Just let me gather my bag," he whispered. He bent down to reach under the bed.

Juniper nodded at Jess. "I'll go help Egg with the next cell."

"Wait—look at this," said Jess, pointing with a frown. There was a sort of trapdoor handle set into the floor. A secret passage? Juniper hurried over, bending for a closer look.

"What is it?" she said, keeping her voice low.

Jess didn't answer.

Juniper looked up. Jess stood over her, and Juniper caught her breath at the other girl's face. Determination and fear and—regret? In the next breath, Jess brought her hand up and flicked all her fingers out wide. Juniper scrabbled backward. She felt a gob of something sticky hit her cheek. She pawed at it, smearing it away and scrambling to her feet as quick as she could.

"Jess?" she whispered. What was going on?

The next instant she felt woozy. Her knees went weak, and the room around her began to spin. She thought of Cyril toppling headfirst, out cold. "What have you done?" Juniper said. But she could already tell the words weren't making it from her brain all the way out her mouth.

The walls tilted sideways, and the dark stone flashed white.

Then the light went out altogether, and Juniper knew nothing at all.

19

JUNIPER AWOKE WITH A START AND A SPLASH
of water up her nose. She jerked upright blinking, her mind as fuzzy
as bindweed. She looked around. She was back in the Aerie, surrounded by a cluster of fearful faces. The early sun shimmered outside the window.

She opened her mouth, croaked, then cleared her throat noisily.

There was a scuffle of feet, then Leena, Tippy, and Erick
crowded into her line of sight.

"O Most Resurrected of All Junipers, you are safe!" said Tippy,
collapsing at her feet in a torrent of sobs.

Everything came back to Juniper in a rush. "Jess?!" she said.
She twisted around to look at the room. Jess was nowhere to be
seen. Neither was Egg. "Where are those girls? Did Jess really use
her . . . her sleeping potion on me?" Juniper's mind was buzzing
with questions, but they all seemed stoppered up inside her throat.
She couldn't get her words out fast or clearly enough.

"You're all right now, Mistress Juniper," said Leena consolingly.

She was sitting right next to her, one hand on Juniper's arm and the other holding out a wet cloth.

"I . . . She knocked me out, didn't she?" Juniper's fingers found her cheek. The gunk was gone.

"She did," said Erick darkly. "Jessamyn Ceward drugged you with some dastardly potion. I've no idea what."

"Scarlet valerian root." Juniper's brain was still fuzzy, but the events in the dungeon were slowly coming back to her. "The same thing she used on Cyril. But *why*?"

"The why is both easy and difficult to answer," said Erick. "Jess is gone, and her father the spy with her."

"And Fleeter! She took Fleeter!" wailed Tippy. "Not even did I get to say good-bye."

"She prepared for this, that much is clear," said Root. "All her belongings are gone—layered inside the pockets of her cloak, no doubt."

"Every last jar and vial," spat Leena.

"I should have guessed something was up when I saw her putting on that heavy cloak. For an indoor mission! In the dead of summer!" Erick slapped his forehead. "So we know the *what*. But the *why*—that, I have no idea."

"But we have someone who does, I'm sure," said a voice from the outer edge of the circle.

That got Juniper to her feet. "Cyril?!" she yelped. Then she wobbled, steadying herself on Leena's arm.

Sure enough, Cyril stood a few steps from the others, looking at her with a mixture of concern, sympathy, and awkward embarrassment. "Um," he said. "Ah. Hullo, Cousin. Can't stop yourself from copying everything I do, eh?"

"Cyril Lefarge, I am in no mood," Juniper snapped. She checked herself for alarm at seeing him untied: She found none. Interesting. Still, she turned to Erick. "Explain, *please*."

Erick nodded. Far from his usual timid manner, he now looked firm and confident. "Cyril woke up shortly after you left. He made it clear that he wanted to talk, so I removed his gag." He added, "It was really just to give him water at first—he also looked parched. But it turned out he . . . had a lot to say. And what he said made sense."

"Chief among the things I wanted to talk about was the untrustworthiness of a certain pair of Ceward sisters."

"What?" said Juniper, plopping down on a cushion. Lands, but her legs had the collywobbles!

Now she saw Egg: Her skinny body was propped on the couch, swathed in the rope bindings and gag formerly used on Cyril. Next to her sat Root, a determined scowl on his face as though she might fly away and he was the only thing keeping her aground.

"That day last week, when I was in the Royal Suite talking with my stepmother and you were spying on me . . . I assume it was you?" Cyril said, lifting an eyebrow. "Who else would make such an infernal racket while trying to be sneaky?"

"Hey!" said Juniper hotly. "That wasn't—I just—" She caught Tippy's eye. "Never mind. Go on."

"At any rate, I figured you all had changed plans and come in early, suspecting me of dastardly deeds. So I kept an eye out. I saw

Tippy right away in the kitchens, and others of you here and there."

Juniper wilted. Had they really been that obvious?

Cyril smiled mischievously, as though reading her mind. "I was *looking* for you specifically. No one else would have suspected a thing—you were all shockingly stealthy."

"So why didn't you say something to us, then, if you had such good intentions?" challenged Root.

Cyril scratched his head. "Ever since I got back here, I've been doing a lot of mulling. And some things didn't add up. Did you read the letters Jess sent her sister?" Juniper shook her head. "I didn't think so. I've got some experience with sneaking and double-crossing myself, and I know things aren't always clear-cut. Most of you were focused on gathering information about my stepmother and the goings-on in the castle, but the Cewards . . . not so much. They seemed to be off doing things on their own. So I figured I would sit tight and see what happened. I didn't want to show my hand too soon if there were unsavory elements within your ranks. Meanwhile, I was plenty busy dogging my stepmother's every move, making sure she didn't mess with my father's health any further, and trying to counteract the damage she's done to him so far. *And* keeping an eye out for my little brother."

"Artie," said Juniper.

"Yeah. He's three. Honestly? He's the main reason I came back when I did. I just . . . " He shook his head. "My stepmother is the most self-centered woman alive. Believe me on this. And my father means well, but he has been under her thumb for as long as he's known her. You think this takeover plan came from his mind?" He barked a laugh. "Not a wisp of it. Oh, he's not guiltless—he went along with it, after all. We both did. And now he's paying the price, for all that I'm trying to counteract her malice."

The knot of questions was so thick in Juniper's mind right now that all she could do was listen, trusting that Cyril would untangle the whole snarl in due time.

"My father's a grown man—I wasn't worried about him." He frowned. "Although apparently I should have been. But Artie—oh, my stepmother does love him, I know. But he's still such a baby. And she gets so involved with herself that she neglects him awfully. I needed to come back and make sure he was all right."

Juniper frowned. "That's your reason?"

"All right, there's more. That night before I left—we were all sitting down together hashing out the big plan. You didn't even take into account my part in things. What do you think would have happened if I showed up right at the same time as you all? You think my stepmother would have trusted a thing I tried to tell her?" He shook his head. "I needed to arrive here on my own, at some space from the rest of the group, if I wanted her to believe I was still on her side." He glared. "And it worked, didn't it? I'm not a bit sorry I did."

"But, Cyril," Juniper said, exasperated, "you could have—well, why didn't you just say all this back in the Basin?"

Cyril shrugged. "You didn't fully trust me, I could tell that. I knew you'd refuse if I asked to leave early." She opened her mouth to protest, but he cut in quickly. "Didn't I offer to go on the scouting expedition? You wouldn't have it. So I couldn't risk this. If you weren't on board, I'd have put my plan out there and lost all chance of sneaking away. And . . . well, maybe a part of me wanted to see if you *would* believe me. I thought to myself, She'll probably imagine the worst, but who knows?"

"You were testing me?"

"I guess I was." Cyril broke into a grin. "If so, then you failed miserably. But in any case, I came back for Artie, and for infiltration, and instead I found this unspeakable business going on with my father."

"He had an accident, I heard," put in Leena. "Fell off a horse and never came back 'round?"

"No chance of that," said Cyril. "I got my hands on the so-called medical records. That doctor is in my stepmother's private employ, and he is *not* there to make my father well. She's keeping him sedated. Among other things."

"But why would she do that?" Juniper said. "Her own husband!"

"Well, she wants the power, pure and simple. *All* the power," said Cyril. "That's what she's always been after. As long as my father was around, he would be gumming up the works, trying to rule the kingdom himself, questioning her decisions. Imagine that! No, she has to have the final word in everything. Always has. Except now it's gone beyond our family to the whole of Torr."

There was a silence.

"All right," Juniper said finally. "So we're caught up, and that brings us to tonight." She glanced at Egg, who was watching the proceedings with a hawkish eye. Judging by her angle on Cyril and the look on her face, she had managed to follow the conversation.

Good. Juniper had a few choice questions for this girl.

The first of which was, if the sisters had finked on them, how was Egg still here?

"Let's untie her," said Juniper, and Leena set to work.

"First I got something to say," Tippy cut in. She scrubbed a hand at her eyes and swallowed thickly. "I understand why you didn't free Elly, My Own Princess Juniper. I know you would have if you could." The girl fought tears again, and Juniper wilted.

"I'm so sorry, Tippy. We never even got as far as the main prison area. I promise we'll find a way back into that dungeon to rescue your sister, and *soon*. But let's get the whole story, shall we?" Tippy wiped her eyes and nodded, and Juniper turned to Root. "Now, what exactly happened after I passed out?"

"I heard movement coming back up the stairs," said Root, "and figured you all were returning—though it was quicker than I expected, and the signals were off, so I hadn't yet diverted the guard as we'd planned. The guard heard the steps, too, and went to the door. Must have figured it was the inside men heading out. He stood right before the door, all casual-like. Instead"—Root swallowed—"instead, the door flung open so hard, it knocked him off his feet. He toppled back, and before he could even yell, a man leaped out holding something in both his hands. He swung at the guard's head, and the guy fell over flat."

Juniper gasped audibly. The others were silent, apparently having heard this story already. "Ceward?" she whispered.

"I didn't know who it was at first, but then I saw Jess right behind him. It was his boot he swung—giant thing, all heavy and hobnailed. He shoved it back on his foot, and they both tore down

155

the hall before I could pick my jaw up off the floor. I didn't know whether to follow them or what, but I decided to come look for you instead. I found you on the ground in the empty cell, with Egg bending over you. I brought her back to the Aerie first—she came with me willingly, I'll add—then Leena and I returned zippy-quick for you. And here we are."

Leena had finished with the knots by now, and Egg rose stiffly to her feet, stretching her arms and legs while her eyes darted from face to face.

"Can you follow our speech without Jess to interpret?" Juniper asked.

Egg fished out her chalk. "Mostly. Can get the general meaning. I have much practice. My father was very"—she smudged something out—"persistent in my spy training."

Juniper folded her arms. "So you double-crossed us."

"*They.* Not me."

"Come on," scoffed Cyril. "I know a thing or two about families and betrayal. Don't tell me you weren't in on this plan."

Root raised his eyebrows at Cyril as if to say, *Tread lightly, my friend.* Cyril wasn't on quite so solid ground yet as to go about pointing accusing fingers. His last remark appeared to hit home, however. Egg pressed her lips together and gave the barest shrug. Then she wrote, "I chose not to go with them."

"Why would you stay?" asked Juniper. "Did you hang back to check on something? Pinch something from my pockets, maybe, before Root caught you?"

Egg shook her head. "I did not agree with them."

Juniper considered this. "Why?"

Egg just shrugged, as if the answer was beneath her.

"Still," Juniper persisted. "Even if that was true. You didn't tell anyone what they were planning to do—you just let them go ahead."

Again Egg shrugged, as if to say, *What would you expect me to do?* "I did not agree with them," she repeated aloud.

"But you weren't going to oppose your family," said Juniper, beginning to understand. She couldn't decide whether to be glad of Egg's loyalty or furious that she hadn't been loyal enough to stop Jess's plan. "But—what *was* Jess's plan, anyway? Are they working with the Mantis?"

Egg shook her head and bent over her armband. "My father takes no sides in politics. Jess has always wanted to impress him. She has succeeded at last."

"And you?" Juniper asked, studying her.

Egg took a deep breath. Juniper saw her hands twitching and wished she could communicate with her in sign language. But the girl persisted, writing on her arm a sentence at a time, then erasing and adding another when all had read. "My father is expert at not getting involved. He wants to stay removed from all parties so he is never tied to any one side. He follows the highest payout, nothing else. I do not follow his view." The last line was underlined. Twice.

"A spy acts alone?" Juniper said quietly.

Egg flicked her gaze away.

"What about that valerian stuff Jess used on me? And on Cyril," Juniper added, seeing his scowl.

Egg's mouth twisted. She scratched some more, then raised her armband.

"Scarlet valerian root tincture," Juniper read. "One of my father's bag of tricks. The boot, too. His heels are lined with lead. I am surprised they imprisoned him to begin with. He is rarely caught off guard."

"And so Jess helped get him out of there," Juniper said, unnecessarily.

Egg wrote on. "My sister has long seen me as her rival for our father's affection. My father put a lot of time into my training. He did not see the same skills in Jess. He always brought me on his spying journeys, not her. So. Jess will be happy now. She has our father's full attention. And I am free of it."

Juniper considered this.

Egg went on. "Another thing: Jess was the one who drugged you. My father would never do something so foolish. The crown princess of Torr!" She rolled her eyes. "But Jess is . . . Jess. And once it was done, he chose to run. They both did." She paused, then wrote with a flourish. She flung her arm up with a defiant toss of her head. "What my father and Jess did was wrong," Juniper read. "What has befallen Torr is wrong. I am at your service."

Juniper looked up and met Egg's gaze, which was proud and flint-hard. "Why?" Juniper said.

After a moment, Egg's fierce look collapsed. "I am"—she paused and looked around—"ready to stop acting alone. I like being part of a team."

"All right," said Juniper. "All right."

"So what's next, then?" asked Leena.

"We head back to the dungeon, that's what!" crowed Tippy.

Root considered. "It's daylight now, but come tonight, who's to stop us? We can venture back and free the prisoners as planned."

Erick cleared his throat. He looked at the ground.

"What now?" said Juniper.

"The Everykey is gone," said Erick at last. "Jess took it with her. *And* the whole bag of gnuts besides. We haven't a way to get back into the dungeons without them."

This left Juniper speechless. She had *taken* the lock pick? That was sheer spite! "Well, can't we find more gnuts? There's got to be more around the palace."

"Sure," said Erick. "We have the diagrams, and Egg has built it once, so it's bound to be easier the second time around. But . . . " He looked at Egg.

"Too long," Egg wrote. "No time."

"Quite right," said Cyril. "Think about it: The Slippery Cewards left some gift-wrapped trouble back in the dungeons. That knocked-out guard? The missing prisoner? By now, the whole castle will be on the alert—not to mention up in arms trying to figure out what's going on. There's only one thing to do."

Cyril looked at each of them in turn, and Juniper hardest of all. "You all need to get out of the palace, quick as you can."

20

JUNIPER STARED AT CYRIL. EGG NARROWED
her eyes and the others started up some angry muttering, but
Juniper cut them off. "Explain," she said to Cyril. "What do you
mean?"

"My stepmother's guards will be scouring the palace from top
to bottom," Cyril explained. "If they find you stowed away up
here, it's all over. Leena and Tippy and Egg are known, as am I.
We can all slide back to our places, and we should do that right
quick, to avoid suspicion. Plus, I need to get back to my father.
I've been away from him long enough, and that devil of a doctor
is due to arrive any time now. But the rest of you need to make
yourselves scarce."

Juniper digested this. That left her and Erick and Root.

"I can get you through the gates," said Cyril, "but you should
stay out for the day. By then the frenzy should have died down. I can
unlock one of the smaller side gates this evening and leave a back
window open for you in the summer kitchen."

"And we're just supposed to let you jaunt on back to your mommy now, are we?" said Leena scornfully. "Trust that you've got our best interests in mind after you've conveniently parceled us out of your way?"

Cyril rolled his eyes, but his hands were clenched. Juniper opened her mouth, then shut it again. What did she *really* think of this plan? To her surprise, the answer was: She trusted Cyril. She really did. She hadn't been sure of it before, and certainly back in the Basin she hadn't trusted him at all. He'd been right about that. But now he'd gone and come back, and he wanted to go again. And maybe it was just time or talk or stupidity, even. But this time she really did believe he was on their side.

"I trust you," Juniper blurted. The words rang out in the room, crisp and sharp-edged and very, very right. "I trust you, Cyril Lefarge. And I think your plan is a sound one. Necessary, even." She turned to face the others. "You know what else I like about this? It gives everyone a day off. I mean it! How can we properly overthrow an enemy kingdom if we're busy collapsing from stress and overwork?"

"But time is everything right now," said Erick.

"I might not have chosen this particular time to go out for a break," Juniper admitted. "But Cyril's right—we can't stay in the palace. If we get caught now, the game's over. So, we could hole up in the Pockets all day, sure. We could sit in there knocking our heads together and legging it from shadows. *Or* we could take a few hours to browse the festival, visit the food stalls, mingle. We'll meet back in the Aerie tonight, and I guarantee by then we'll have a new and better plan, *and* a groundswell of energy to carry it off."

The necessary plan might have been out there somewhere, but over the rest of that day it proved wickedly hard to find. While they slipped through the Pockets and out into the balmy summer air, Juniper kept her eyes wide and her mind open. As she ruffled her short hair and pulled the brim of her cap down farther over her face, as she nibbled on a web of spun sugar, as she challenged Root against a ball-toss merchant, her mind never stopped whirring. Not for a single moment.

"Over here!" Erick called. "Butterfight!"

Juniper pushed through the crowds, with Root close behind her. The butterfight was a high point of the yearly Summerfest: One was held each day of the festival. Traditionally, the fighters had donned their customary rompers and greased themselves from head to toe in actual butter before stepping into the wrestling ring. But these days, lard was always used: It made for a greasier and more slippery finish, was less likely to go rancid in the heat, more cost-effective, *and* it left the wrestlers with a glowing complexion besides.

The sun was high overhead. Just below it, the Glassroom gleamed like an evil second sun, though the king had retired behind his privacy curtains and could not be seen. The upper crown of the dome had been swung open for ventilation, but it still had to be stiflingly hot in there. How long could her father survive in such conditions? The beauty of the day turned to ash as Juniper fought back tears.

She would get him out of there—she *would*.

"And they're down!" came the bellow from the butterfight ring. The crowd pushed in closer, then groaned back as a wave of warm lard splattered over the faces and fronts of those who had gone too close—which was nearly the whole crowd, since the ring was a wide oblong.

Juniper blinked once. Twice. Then again.

She'd just had an idea.

When the sun started to set, the little group crept around to the narrow side entrance Cyril had specified. The door in the bluevines had been left unlocked and they piled inside. They tiptoed across the lawns, clambered into the summer kitchen window, and eased through the Pockets to their nest in the Aerie.

Intruders had been here, that was clear. Cushions had been overturned and furniture moved. The ghost bats were chittering at twice their normal volume, and Tippy stood near their cubbies, sending a soothing string of babble their way. Leena was running around straightening the disordered room, while Egg and Cyril stood frowning, hands on their hips.

"What's the story?" Juniper asked Cyril. "Will the guards keep on searching?"

Cyril shrugged. "Hard to say. But I'm thinking no. Since the one actual dungeon escapee was that slippery spy, they feel he had special help breaking out and is long gone. They guess he's not connected to a bigger threat."

"That's some good news," said Leena.

"Honestly?" said Cyril. "I think my stepmother has bigger fish to gut right now. As long as those who matter are still locked up tight, she's not too worried."

"All right," said Juniper. The guards had been and gone. Their day of hiding in plain sight had been worth it. And Cyril was still firmly on their side; her trust in him had paid off. They were safe—for the moment. But her father was still in his lighted cell. And deep in the dungeons were Erick's father and Tippy's sister and countless others whom Juniper had not been able to save.

Suddenly the pressure, the weight of all that needed doing and the obstacles stacked against them and the many who would suffer if they failed—who were suffering, right now—suddenly, it all felt like too much. The responsibility was like a giant thumb pressing down on Juniper's head, and all she wanted to do was crawl under her covers and block out the world.

Eventually they had talked themselves out and put the room back into some semblance of order, and everyone collapsed onto their sleeping piles. Even Cyril was too tired to head back to his room and pronounced himself ready for a good old-fashioned Queen's Basin sleepover. But long after the others had sunk to snoozing, Juniper stayed wide-eyed, tossing restlessly from one edge of her folded quilt to the other. Finally the pale light of dawn started scratching at the horizon and she gave up and rose. Putting both hands on the open window, she leaned out to breathe deeply of the scented predawn air. Beyond the walls, the Bazaar was still quiet and mostly dark at this early hour—Summerfest Day 3 looming on the horizon—with only dim lights bobbing in the sleeping field as early risers prepared their wares for the day ahead. Across the castle grounds burned the light of the ever-glowing Glassroom. Her father's prison chamber.

Juniper clenched her fists. It wasn't fair. Why should deception and betrayal and scheming machinations win the day? Why not truth and loyalty and hard work?

Her eyes blurred with tears as she gazed at the glowing prison cell. And then she blinked. And looked again, closer this time. Through the glass walls, the rare flowers that grew inside could clearly be seen. Before, they had been a tangled riot of blues and reds and yellows. Now the yellow and the red were there in abundance. But the blue . . .

Juniper caught her breath. How had she not seen this immediately? All around the inside of the glass dome swung a huge, elaborate wreath made entirely of cornflower-blue blossoms. The blue banner wrapped all the way around the walls, bold and bright and true.

It was the same exact shade of blue as the stone Juniper had sent her father.

Now the tears came freely. He'd gotten her message; he got it, and he answered it in the only way he could. He knew she was out here. He knew she was coming.

This game wasn't over, not by a long shot.

They might be few and frail. They might be pressed down by all the thumbs of all the giants in the world, but it didn't matter. Nothing mattered. Juniper Torrence was playing to win.

In the still-dark room, she strode over and scratched the starter stones until the lamp flared up hot and yellow. Tousled heads lifted around the room, sleepy eyes blinking open, mouths stretching into grumpy yawns.

Juniper smiled a little—there was a special thrill to waking up a group of sleepy friends—then clapped loudly. "Are we beaten?" she called.

There was a silence, then Leena croaked, "If I say yes, can we go back to sleep?"

Cyril rolled over and pulled the covers farther over his head. "What foolhardy plan made me stay here overnight?"

"Oh! Oh!" cried Tippy, leaping up, instantly wide awake. "I know the answer to this one! Can I say it?"

"Say away," said Juniper, grinning and poking Cyril's back with her foot. "Listen up, Cousin. Are we beaten, do you suppose?"

"NOOOO!" bellowed Tippy, so loudly that Juniper exchanged a startled glance with Erick and they both looked furtively at the trapdoor that led to the main palace.

"Quite right," Juniper said quickly. "We are not beaten, not even close to it. Our plans may have been thwarted, but what of it?"

"There's a rank lot more plans where that came from, I reckon," said Cyril dryly, sitting up with a yawn.

"Fling the heralds!" Leena groused. "The lad is actually *right* for once."

Cyril sighed and threw off his covers, reaching into the knapsack he'd stowed by his rolled-up quilt. He pulled something out of a pouch and started sneaking looks into his palm. What was he . . . *oh*, Juniper realized, as Cyril turned the tiny looking glass from side to side, inspecting his teeth and smoothing his sticking-up hair. At another time, she would have seized the chance to tease him, but not today. Let Cyril primp and get himself into top form.

It was show day.

"Thirty-six hours," Juniper said a short time later, as they all sat gathered in a rough circle, picking through a hastily assembled breakfast of leftovers Egg had siphoned from dinner the night before. Pausing for a moment with a day-old cucumber sandwich in her hand (which managed to be both dry and soggy at the same time), Juniper reflected on how she had gone from eating delicacies on gilded bone china to passing around a beaten copper tray of the maids' leavings. She hungrily picked up another and started a new mental list: *Delicious Things to Eat Once We Get My Father's Throne Back.*

It was a long list.

"Thirty-six hours," Juniper repeated, coming back to herself as she discarded a sandwich corner that was just too stale for comfort. Food was well and good, but right now she needed to focus. "That's how much time we have left. That's when the Monsian delegation arrives with whatever army they bring along. Shortly after that, the Mantis will crown herself queen. And after *that*"—she swallowed—"my father will be carted off to a proper prison somewhere too far for us ever to save him."

"What can we do, though?" asked Leena. "We've had any number of plans and ideas, and we keep tripping headlong over traitors and roadblocks of every type."

Across the circle came a loud snort. Cyril said, "When's a good old-fashioned traitor ever stopped you lot before?"

Juniper startled, but when she caught her cousin's gaze, there was nothing in it but grudging admiration. Deep in her gut, some last tightly bound thread cut loose. She met his slow smile with her own.

"But you've got a new plan for us, don'tcha?" asked Tippy anxiously.

"Undoubtedly," said Erick. "Princess Juniper makes lists and plans for her lists and plans. She's probably spinning a half dozen right now as we speak."

Juniper grinned. "I thought you'd never ask. Now, it just so happens that I *do* have a new idea. It's awful risky, though."

"As the best ones are," said Cyril.

"Indeed. It's going to take a lot of work besides, *and* some creative thinking, which is bound to be fun." She looked around the circle at each of them in turn. "Are we all ready for a little energetic mayhem?" To their enthusiastic nods, she leaned closer. "It's going to be good, but there's some preparation to be done beforehand. Listen up, and I'll tell you all about it."

21

THAT MORNING FLEW BY. TIPPY, LEENA, AND Cyril kept to their palace work duties, dealing as usual with those around them to avoid raising any suspicion, as well as keeping their ears open for any new information to help the cause. Meanwhile, Juniper, Egg, Erick, and Root plotted and schemed and kept busy with the preparations needed to turn their rough-carved plan into a gleaming work of art.

Or something like that.

"Where's Paul?" asked Root at one point, as they sat together in the Aerie. "He's not been with the Bobcats for days."

"He's gone to the Anju, right?" said Erick.

"I believe Zetta is good for her word," said Juniper with a nod. "She promised to send help if we needed it, and we couldn't need a fighting force more than we do right now. Whether she can get her people to follow her to the lowlands—after all of our history—is another story. But I'm hopeful."

Before she could say more, the Aerie door slapped open.

"Monsians!" gasped Tippy. "For the love of everything, they're *here*!"

Juniper leaped to her feet. *What?* The Monsian delegation wasn't expected until tomorrow, and she'd been rather hoping that they would fulfill their reputation for poor scheduling and show up even later.

Instead, they were a day *early*?!

The whole group flocked to the north-side windows. They looked over the palace rooftops; past the gardens, mazes, and outbuildings; over the walls; and up the White Highway leading away into the distance. Far, far up the Highway, swathed in clouds of white dust, they could just make out the tall flags and banners flaunting the Monsian crest. Behind that was a hint of horseflesh and a flash of gilded carriage. Beyond that, the rest of the column wound away into the distance.

The Monsians.

It was too far to tell for sure, but they seemed to have spread over the whole roadway, as though no one else was of any importance. Juniper wondered how many wagons, horse riders, and pedestrians were being forced into the weeds while the troops marched past.

"The gall of them!" said Erick. "They act like they own this country."

Juniper's stomach hurt just watching them. There was one good thing, though: They were still a long way out. "We've got time yet," she said. "But how much, I have no idea."

Erick tilted his head and pondered. "They won't be here before nightfall. That's a long road, and look how packed it is with people and carts. Moving all that out of the way in front of them will make for a very slow march."

"So, tomorrow morning, you reckon?"

"Midday at the latest."

"Very well, then," said Juniper. "Challenge accepted. We have until nightfall to win this game."

"We're just moving things forward by a day," Juniper insisted an hour later. The time for caution was long past, they had decided, and all undercover Goshawk members had abandoned their roles in the palace. They were now clustered in the Aerie, bent over various tasks needed to launch their plan: mixing, sewing, packing, planning. Today was the first of four grand feast days, all of which would culminate in the final end-of-Summerfest bash inside the palace. They'd planned to use today to gather information and logistics: how things would be run, where the Mantis would sit, how Bobcat would perform their routine. But— "Now we're down to real push-and-shove. All we can do is plunge in and hope for the best."

It was scant comfort. But they'd been out on a limb before. Indeed, as Juniper's father had often quipped, that was the best place to find the fruit.

"So here's what we should expect this afternoon," Juniper announced, while her hands kept busy working. "A string of tables are even now being set up along the length of the entryway leading in toward the Small Gardens."

171

Tippy danced up on the very tips of her toes and whooped in delight.

Juniper grinned. "All those smells you've been pining for? And helping work on, like as not? The tables shall soon be food-stuffed into tomorrow morning: meat pies and fruit tarts and cheese twists aplenty, fresh fruit bowls, loads of vegetables for munching. Pots of cream. Chocolate squares. Almond sponge fingers. Tiny crystal cups of sherbet. Oh, Tippy, just you wait!"

"Shall we have time to graze a bit, then? All the while we're saving the kingdom-like?"

"There's always time for good food," Juniper said. "Though we'll have to eat on the run, for there's that much to do!"

"I know, I know," said Tippy. "Time's a-ticking, and the Monsians won't wait."

"So we're really doing this," said Leena, in the tone of a personal pep talk.

"We are," said Juniper. She took the heavy bowl that Egg had been mixing, sniffed it approvingly, then began to carefully pour the slurry into the waterproofed satchel in her lap. "How's it looking out there?" she called to Root.

Root took a long look out the window, then wobbled his hands. "The grounds are still pretty sparse, but it looks like the gates are being opened."

"Finally," said Erick.

"I'm surprised the Mantis is letting the commoners in at all," said Leena.

"She can't bar them from Summerfest altogether," said Cyril.

"How would that look? She managed to keep them out of the palace proper, and she's cutting the numbers down on those let in the grounds. But I wouldn't be surprised if she finds other ways to trim corners. We'll want to get out there just as soon as we can, get things under way."

Juniper nodded. "Let's give the courtyards another hour to fill up, then we'll venture out. Grab a few goodies as we go"—she grinned at Tippy, who pumped a fist in the air—"then head straight to the Bobcats' wagon, which will be in the Small Gardens with the other performers. Then we get ready for showtime."

"Showtime!" The yell came from Leena, who seemed to surprise herself nearly as much as she did the others.

"To victory!" said Cyril, and thrust a hand, palm out, into the center of the group. Juniper caught his eye, grinned, and slapped her hand on his. One by one, the others brought their hands to meet in the middle, palms on fingers on fists, in one glorious, determined huddle.

First, the Aerie. Then, the castle.

Showtime.

22

BY THE TIME THE FRIENDS BEGAN MAKING their stealthy way to the courtyard, the place was swarming. The doors to the palace proper had been barred off, along with the whole back of the castle grounds: the orchards and gardens, the stables, and the army barracks. The front half, though, was teeming with festivalgoers. Villagers, courtiers, merchants, and bare-legged ragamuffin children ran wild in a higgledy-piggledy mishmash. Moving amongst them, Juniper felt a fierce rush of pride and joy. It was almost possible to forget, in the ordinary whirl of this familiar and most beloved of holidays, all that was wrong behind the scenes.

Almost. But not quite.

Through the crowds of commoners and scattered nobles marched armed guards, stern and focused, their eyes alert for any signs of threat. They did not wear the familiar purple and silver colors of Torr—apparently the Mantis had kept the seamstresses busy rustling up brand-new uniforms on short notice.

Now the unfortunate soldiers were bedecked in a garish pastiche of puce-on-black, looking rather like beetles in brightly painted carapaces.

The friends rounded a bend, where Juniper dodged a pair of ruffians fighting over a loaf of bread and pushed past a hedge into her favorite place on the grounds: the Small Gardens. A stage had been erected in front of the marble fountain, which was elaborately decked out with fresh flower garlands and painted gold trim. A low stair curved the waist-high climb to its sleek surface.

Still, so much in the gardens was familiar. Memories flashed across Juniper's mind, lightning quick. This was the fountain where she had played as a tiny child with her mother, their special place to set aside their royal robes on late summer nights and lose themselves in the cool dappled water. This was the courtyard where she and Erick had waited anxiously all those weeks ago to see if any young recruits would join her expedition to start a brand-new, all-kids country. And this was the long gravel roadway that led from the Small Gardens to the front palace gates, along which the magnificent table of delicacies would be set up.

The group ducked in together one final time, just out of sight of the crowds beyond the edge of the maze. Then Egg gave a conspiratorial nod, tapped her shoulder to indicate the bulky lump stuffed under her cloak, then dove into the throngs.

"This is where we part ways as well," murmured Cyril. "I have to go see to Artie. Don't do anything foolhardy in my absence."

"Godspeed, Cousin," Juniper said, squeezing his arm briefly. They all had their places in the kerfuffle to come. It was reassuring to know that someone on the other side would be there to watch her back.

As Cyril moved out into the crowd, he threw back his head and shoulders, like a tall crisp banner unfurling itself in the wind, as though he were suddenly taking up twice as much space in the world as before.

"How does he do that?" said Leena, and Juniper grinned.

"I almost miss the days when I could count him as my rival. He did make such a delicious bad guy." Juniper reached back to grab Tippy's hand. "Come on, Tiplet. Let's go grab us a few treats—but we can't be long, mind! The performances begin at noon, so we must be all of us in the Bobcat wagon by the stroke of ten." She peered up at the timepiece in the marble fountain's base. "That's less than a half hour off."

"Where's all them goodies, then?" said Tippy, a quaver in her voice.

"It don't look half normal out there," said Leena under her breath.

Now that they drew her attention to it, Juniper immediately saw that they were right. The crowds were there aplenty, cut through with jugglers and entertainers and, of course, the ubiquitous guards. Merchants wandered around with tiny table-fronts strapped to their shoulders, boards that yawned out flat and held lunch meats, breads, and sweet pastries. Others circulated with an ornate jug in one hand and a pewter mug in the other, with a wiping rag discreetly tucked in a back pocket.

But one thing that was hugely, glaringly absent was the

extra-long table crammed with free food for the masses. Tippy started hopping foot to foot in distress, as though jumping higher might help her locate the missing treats.

"What is with all the merchants roaming everywhere?" said Root.

"Hmm," said Leena. "Something dastardly is afoot."

Dastardly was a bit strong. But one thing was very clear: The tables of free food were nowhere in sight. In their place, apparently, were a slew of merchants brought in from the Bazaar to sell their own wares—and at quite a high markup, if Juniper was any judge. A little boy in front of them reached chubby hands out for a pewter mug, but the waxy-faced matron with the lemonade jug rubbed her fingers together to show that he wasn't getting something for nothing. The child started to cry, and a weather-beaten farmwife behind him looked embarrassed and yanked the boy away by the arm, clearly unable to pay the drink merchant's fee.

"It's all supposed to be free," said Juniper faintly. "It's our gift to the people! The feasting is the very heart of Summerfest. I don't understand!"

She did, though. How could she not? This was not her father's Summerfest. This was the new kingdom of Malvinia Lefarge. The Mantis had fought for her wealth and power, and she evidently would not relinquish one drop more of it than she had to.

Juniper patted her skirts and pulled out two gold coins. "Tippy," she whispered. "How would you like to put your sneaking skills to good use?" She bobbed her head toward the crying boy, now draped over the shoulder of his faint-looking mother.

Tippy's face lit up. She swiped the coins from Juniper and ducked through the crowd, skittering over feet and under elbows and across sketchy puddles of goo. Reaching the disheveled pair, Tippy dramatically bumped into the farmwife so that she tripped over her own feet. It was a bit over-the-top, Juniper thought, watching out of the corner of her eye, but the woman didn't seem put out. Tippy picked herself up, acting out an elaborate apology, then scurried off into the crowd.

It took a long few minutes before the woman's face turned a violent red, then she blanched. She brought her hands up and peered at them intently. Immediately she jumped up and started scanning the crowds. She looked again at her hand, disbelieving, then shoved it into her pocket. Tucking her child firmly under her arm—he'd now fallen asleep—she pushed off through the crowd.

"A good meal for her now," said Leena with satisfaction. "Well done, Your Majesty."

"Don't call me that!" hissed Juniper. "Not here, where anyone might hear." She pulled the hood of her cloak down farther over her face. Haircut and disguise notwithstanding, her face was nearly as familiar as the king's. If anyone recognized her, it was all over.

"Look at her, though," said Erick. "She doesn't look to be going for food at all."

Sure enough, the determined farmwife was plowing through the crowds, studying every face and turning from side to side in a brisk, businesslike fashion.

"Oh, no," said Juniper. "She's looking for the Tipster, isn't she?"

Erick sighed. "She thinks Tippy dropped those coins by mistake. She wants to give them back."

"I think she's spotted her," said Leena.

The woman now picked up speed and started to yell over the crowd, waving her hands in visible distress.

"She's drawing attention," said Erick.

Tippy had noticed now. She seemed rattled, unsure what to do at this unexpected pursuit. Changing course, she began, disastrously, to beeline it back in their direction.

"No, you fool!" Leena groaned, though of course Tippy was too far off to hear. "Juniper, she's leading them straight to us."

Tippy was nimble and speedy, but the woman was a force of righteous restitution. She simply barreled through all obstacles and kept up.

Juniper suddenly knew what she had to do.

"You grab Tippy," she whispered to Erick, tugging him along with her. "I'll handle the do-gooder."

Juniper melted after Erick into the crowd, where she saw him enfold Tippy in both arms and magic her into a throng of energetic high-kick dancers. Just ahead the woman stopped, blinking, to look around. Her gaze was steely and determined.

She wouldn't give this up. Juniper sighed. So be it.

Juniper stopped abruptly, and the woman came up short to keep from crashing into her back. The farmwife was a touch taller, so Juniper had to tilt her head slightly to look up into the lined, careworn face. Leaning in very close, Juniper pushed her hood back a smidge.

The woman first frowned, then opened her mouth, then her face went pale. "You—but you—are you—"

"Shhh," Juniper said, raising a finger to her lips. "The coins were a gift from me. For you to keep."

The woman's head whipped from side to side, and Juniper thought she couldn't have looked more obvious if she'd tried. "But aren't you away in—" She couldn't seem to form a complete sentence.

"I need your help," said Juniper desperately. "Can I trust you? Nobody must know I am here. *Nobody.* You can't say a word about me—do you hear? Not to anyone."

The woman's eyes widened and her mouth gaped like a fish. She shifted the sleeping child to a better spot on her shoulder.

"Take the coins, please, with my blessing. Buy some food and drink for yourself and the boy. And then"—she swallowed—"then you should go home. I don't know exactly how things are going to unfold here. It may not be safe. But whatever you do, you must not tell a soul that you have seen me."

With that, Juniper pulled her milky cloak tighter around her shoulders and ducked sideways into the crowd. When she glanced back over her shoulder, the farmwife still stood rooted in place. A single tear coursed down her cheek.

23

EVENTUALLY, THE FRIENDS FOUND THEMSELVES tucked safely in the Bobcats' garish wagon. Alta, Toby, Sussi, Filbert, Roddy, and Oona were all very busy stretching and squatting and limbering up, so that Juniper felt like she'd fallen into a bin of living yo-yos. Egg was introduced to the Bobcats, and in her characteristic way she blended easily into the group, studying their warm-up moves with visible delight. To her own joy, Juniper found that a great portion of the roof was made of strong, supple leather, and could be folded all the way back through a system of bars and levers. With the ceiling opened wide to the glorious blue sky, and a large bowl of coriander-spiced popped corn to munch on, things quickly started looking up.

"Do you think that woman will keep quiet about seeing you?" Alta asked.

"You saw that, did you?" said Juniper, her lips twisting.

Alta shrugged. "I was on the lookout. I don't think it was noticeable enough to draw a wider view, though."

"Still," said Erick, "it wasn't a safe thing to do, Juniper."

"We're just lucky no one saw," said Leena. "The crowd is full of poor people who can't afford the treats for sale. If you go about outing yourself to all of them, they're going to be a lot worse off in the long run."

"I know," said Juniper. "I didn't mean for it to happen. It's just—that little tyke looked so dejected. I couldn't stand by and do nothing." She sighed. "At any rate, it's behind us, and what will be will be. If it comes to the worst, we'll deal with it then. Now, how goes the show, Bobcats? What remains to be done?"

"Not a single thing!" said Sussi, beaming with delight. "Only, you should see our act, Princess Juniper. Only, you should see it!"

"She will see it, you dolt," said Oona, but her tone was gentle. "That's the whole point of this, innit?"

Sussi colored. "Well," she said lamely.

Root pulled the satchel off his back and handed it to Alta. "The final materials are in here."

Juniper lowered her voice. "You will find it all just as we discussed, Alta. Keep to the planned timing on your side with the performance, and I think we can pull this off. You have heard the Monsians are on the way?"

"It's the only thing anyone's talking about," said Toby. "You'd think that would turn the people against this impostor, but . . ." He shrugged.

"Never underestimate the power of the masses to follow blindly," said Erick.

"So, the show is ready," Juniper said. "We Goshawks know our places and are ready to spring to action. I daresay . . . we may have done all we can do."

Alta nodded briskly. "We are fifth in the performance lineup, which is due to start at any moment. That puts us—what? Two hours in?"

"Probably less," said Roddy. "I've been roving and listening—most of the shows run no more than a quarter of an hour."

"Very well," said Juniper. "We'd all best get in our places, then. Shall we?"

"Let the war begin," whispered Oona, her eyes gleaming.

"To the war, to win!" said Egg in a loud, clear voice. As she looked challengingly around the circle, Juniper couldn't tell if Egg had misread Oona's lips, or if she'd changed the call deliberately.

Either way. "To the war," whispered Juniper, and lifted her hand high in the air.

"To win!" chorused the group in one joint whispered promise.

While the Balancing Bobcats began changing into their costumes for the coming show, the Goshawks leaned up to the narrow wagon windows and watched the goings-on outside. The first performance was from a group of family singers: a father, mother, grandmother, and no fewer than eight children, ranging from teenagers down to a bowlegged toddler, all draped across the stage in order of height. Each brandished their own instrument, from viola to sackbut to triangle to a memorably off-key kazoo. Several of the group sang throatily; others warbled as the group

183

made its way through six resounding numbers. It was a feast for the eyes, if not always the ears, and that was as much as Juniper could say about that.

They were followed by a mediocre magician; then a storyteller who had some great yarns to spin but couldn't project his voice, and so the crowd yawned and shifted in place; and lastly a trio of clowns—Larabelle, Rainbow, and Silly Lillie—whose brightly painted faces and wildego ways had the onlookers in stitches. They were a hard act to follow, but the enthusiastic response had drawn the whole crowd close to the stage, which Juniper noted with approval from her viewing window.

"Be ready," she whispered to Alta. "We don't want any time to pass between them and us. We can't lose the crowd."

"I've got this," said Filbert, and Juniper looked in surprise at the stolid boy with the earnest face.

"All right, then," she said. "Goshawks—let's head out and leave the Bobcats to their spotlight." The crew gathered up their necessary items and slipped into the crowd.

The stage had been set up with a large, ornate throne on its far left side, so the Mantis could have an uninterrupted view. Juniper half expected Cyril to have wrangled a way onto the stage next to her, but she finally spotted him in the first row of the audience. Tiny tousle-haired Artie bobbed on his shoulders, clapping chubby hands in loud delight at the show.

The moment the clowns left the stage, to uproarious applause, Team Bobcat was ready. Alta, Roddy, Filbert, Toby, Sussi, and

Oona had changed into tightly fitting costumes, each more eye-poppingly bright than the last. The tunics came up high in the neck and ended in matching gloves and booties with built-in toe grips. Juniper was frankly impressed as the group took the stage lugging a variety of chairs, ladders, planks, hoops, and a giant basket stuffed with still more colorful garments.

Juniper grinned. This was going to be one for the books! She was just glad that her current part in the drama involved the *off-stage* action.

As he'd promised, Filbert took the stage first. Reaching into the basket, he solemnly took out a heap of scarlet and purple, which he shrugged over his shoulders to form a sort of feathered shawl. It fell over his arms like wings. He then tugged a yellow cap on his head, pulling it down so it covered the lower half of his face, jutting out into a bright yellow beak.

Juniper clapped a hand over her mouth. She hadn't seen *this* in their practice sessions!

Filbert's huge announcer's voice boomed out of the beak-opening: "Ladies and gentlemen, I am delighted to present for your pleasure the Balancing Bobcats' Birds of Paradise." He bowed deeply to a scattered applause. "While my fellow Bobcats set up for the show, I shall begin . . . with a song." With no further preamble, Filbert opened his mouth.

And the world fell away. The voice that rose from him was a clear, high soprano, projecting through his beak like the crystal sound of a viola on its highest strings. It was an old court song, a mournful ballad about a king who went off to war to save his true love, only to find she had betrayed him for another. King Regis had loved this song, and Juniper fought back tears.

To keep focus, she studied the crowd, but there was no need for concern: They were enraptured, swaying to the sound of Filbert's a cappella magic. The Mantis was unmoved by the performance, and something about the narrowed pinch of her face, the way her gaze flicked ever so slightly toward the glimmering Glassroom, told Juniper that they should be careful. Too much about the virtue (and betrayal) of kings could easily push this performance in the wrong direction. But her expression didn't devolve further, and minutes later, the song was over.

The ramshackle balancing structure was now set in place. Sussi perched high on one side and Toby on the other, with Alta and Roddy holding the bases steady, and Oona standing proudly on the ground between them.

Team Bobcat's performance began.

24

THERE WAS NO DOUBT ABOUT IT: THE BALANCING
Bobcats were spectacular. Juniper had seen fragments of their
practice sessions during the day—and from a distance during
their tryouts—but nothing had prepared her for the full range of
their skills. The tricks were simple, Alta had declared, variations
of the training she herself had undergone in learning her soldiering
skills, only shot through with a lot more climbing, balancing, and
whirling through the air. They'd had some lessons from the
costume-merchant-turned-squid-trawler, too; it seemed he had
been something of an amateur tumbler. All of this Juniper knew,
but she was still unprepared for how vivid they looked in their
colorful feather vests, swirling and toppling and hurtling through
the space as though they themselves were made of air.

It was breathtaking.

Through all this, Juniper and Team Goshawk stayed firmly
wedged in the crowd. Every few minutes, Oona scurried to the
edges of the stage, reaching into a thin leather satchel hooked

around her waist to toss out a handful of wrapped candies. The eager onlookers pushed in closer each time, and Juniper and the others did their best to encourage the rush, while still staying as far back as they could.

On her throne, the Mantis stifled a yawn behind one languid hand. She flicked her gaze toward the fountain's timepiece, apparently less enchanted with the performance than were her subjects. She crooked a hand and an attendant scurried over. She leaned to speak in his ear. Juniper caught Oona's eye. She closed her hand into a fist. Oona nodded imperceptibly.

It was time for the final act.

"Ladies and gentlemen," said Filbert a moment later in his booming voice, "we are proud to present you with our final number."

Oona tossed the last two handfuls of sweets into the crowd. Then she doffed her empty pouch, bowed grandly, and pulled a second, nearly identical pouch out of the costume basket. This pouch was not empty but full, bulging tightly and secured firmly at the top. Juniper flexed her aching fingers at remembering all the frantic work that gone into preparing it.

With a flourish, backed by the final spins and twirls from the others, Oona tied the bag to a long, flexible pole, which she passed to Filbert and he hefted up straight.

"Gather in close, my good audience," he said in a merry singsong. He lifted the pole and began to twirl it dramatically, while the other Bobcats pirouetted and tumbled nearby on their own supports. It was a grand sort of dance, heightened by the musical drumbeat that Filbert now provided as he worked his part of the routine.

The audience pushed in closer, hooting and cheering.

The Mantis raised an eyebrow; maybe the crowd seemed a touch too enthusiastic for her liking? She motioned to her guards. They began to gather around the edges of the crowd, jostling to get closer to the stage. In Juniper's peripheral vision, she saw Cyril tug Artie off his back and twist away with him.

Filbert raised his voice to a higher pitch, which sent the audience into a frenzy. Someone let out a shriek.

"Enough!" The Mantis jumped to her feet, flashed a hand at her attendants, and spun to leave the stage.

This was it: the moment of truth.

From behind Juniper came the barely audible sound of a *twang*. Egg melted into the side bushes, and Juniper knew her bow and arrow would already be tucked safely back into the holster beneath her cloak.

Meanwhile, the slender arrow cut through the air, arcing over the heads of the crowd to pierce the center of the bulging bag, which still spun in circles on the end of Filbert's stick.

The arrow sank through the thin hide.

The bag . . . exploded.

Juniper dropped to her knees in the crowd and threw her cloak over her head. She hoped the other Goshawks had been in time to do the same. Through her crouch she heard the loud, wet *squelch* of an overfull container bursting in midair and midswing. Then with a gentle *burp*, the contents disgorged.

This bag was not full of candies. This bag was jam-full of something much wetter, much slimier.

Much more *useful*.

Juniper stayed hidden as the noises around her went from shock to alarm to a series of faint thuds. Then she jumped up. Faces and arms of the bystanders all around her were spattered in goo. The empty bag now hung, deflated, at the end of the pole. Raucous crowd and overbearing soldiers alike—all of whom had pushed in so close to the stage—had been generously pelted with Rogett Ceward the Spymaster's scarlet valerian sleeping potion. Each person was now slumped over, insensible, one atop the other, all comatose limbs and uncoordinated bodies. On the stage, Malvinia Lefarge lay sprawled as well. Team Bobcat—with their gloved hands and masked faces—were the only ones in motion, wiping gunk from their outfits and clambering off the stage in her direction.

Juniper felt a pang for all these innocent sleepers, but they would come around in a few hours, with nothing worse than a mild headache and cramped limbs from being sprawled out in a heap.

This Juniper knew from experience.

Her biggest concern right now was to seize the moment and do what they were here to do. She looked around quickly. Every soldier on duty in the Small Gardens had been either guarding the Mantis or patrolling the crowd. Every one was now down for the count. Thank goodness for small glories! Of course, there were plenty more soldiers inside the palace.

They needed to move quickly.

The few villagers and merchants who had been far enough back from the stage to escape the slumber-potion were scurrying away toward the castle gates, just as fast as their legs would carry them. It looked like all the nobles and dignitaries had used their stations to acquire front-row seats; none of them had come through unscathed.

Then a loud voice cut through Juniper's thoughts. "GUARDS! What in the name of nightfall is going on here?!"

To her horror, Juniper turned back to the stage to see the Mantis rising to her feet, face crimson and shoulders shaking with rage. She'd started walking away just before the bag burst, Juniper remembered. She'd had her back turned. And with the thickness of her robes and headdresses—of course. The Mantis hadn't gotten more than a sprinkling of the potion: enough to make her momentarily drowsy or dizzy. But now she was wide awake once again, and on the warpath.

The one person they *needed* to subdue had been missed entirely.

"GUARDS!" the Mantis roared. "To me!"

25

HALFWAY DOWN THE STAGE HEADING TOWARD Juniper, Alta froze in place. She looked back toward the Mantis. She looked at Juniper. What should they do—push forward, or retreat? How much could they hope to accomplish if the Mantis was not unconscious along with the others? If they all ran now, Juniper reasoned, they could probably make it out of the castle grounds and hide away well enough to plot a proper escape.

But then what? If they failed at their mission, if they couldn't reclaim the palace, couldn't save her father, what was left to do?

Juniper spun in a quick circle. The rest of Team Bobcat had begun picking their way across the felled bodies toward her. The scattered Goshawks were still dragging themselves up off the ground or wriggling from under fallen townspeople. All seemed awake and in motion. Egg slunk out of the far edge of the maze and stood surveying the wreckage, hands on her hips.

Well. In the end, it was a choice that made itself. Why else were they here, after all? Were they the type of fighters who gave up after one setback?

Bringing her fingers to her lips, Juniper let out one earsplitting whistle.

They certainly were not.

The piercing sound caromed across the eerily silent square. Once Juniper had all her settlers' attention (including a stiff wave for Egg), she brought both hands high in the air.

"Phase two!" she yelled, and everyone sprang into motion.

"What IS going on here? GUARDS!" Malvinia bellowed again.

But . . . no guards were coming. Not yet, anyway. The ones within earshot were all down for the count.

Juniper nodded to Alta, who sprang back up onto the stage. As she went, Alta snagged one of the long, flexible balancing poles, which she brandished at the Mantis like a very dull, bendy sword.

Then Juniper felt a thump on her back. Before she could register what was happening, there was a warm, squirming bundle in her arms. Cyril jogged her shoulder. "Watch this little gimlet for me, will you? I'm off to do something foolhardy."

Without giving Juniper a chance to reply, Cyril sprinted over, across, and through the sea of felled bodies. He reached the stage and vaulted to the top, flinging up his cloak to expose his scabbard. With one smooth *swish*, his sword was in his hand. He arced it around and pointed it straight at his stepmother.

The Mantis had not so much as blinked an eye at Alta's affront, but now her eyebrows met her hairline. "Cyril?" she said. "What are you about? What is that sword for?"

"This sword," said Cyril bitingly, "is for your attack on the country of Torr, for your betrayal of your rightful king, *and* for your thinking to dispose of my father in the same callous way."

She started to shake her head, but Cyril snapped, "Don't even bother denying it. We're not here to talk, Stepmother. Alta, would you mind terribly if I took over here? It's gotten rather personal, you understand."

Alta nodded and grabbed a length of rope. "I'll go take care of the guards. We don't know how much of the potion they got or when they'll start coming around."

"Ceepee!" came a burble from Juniper's arms, and she looked down, aghast. She'd been so caught up in the activities onstage that she just now realized she was holding an actual breathing child.

"Oh, lands!" she groaned. "Cyril left me his half brother. What in the name of everything am I going to do with a baby?"

"Ceepee!" sang Artie.

"Hiya, pal!" chirped a voice behind her, and Juniper wilted in relief.

"Tippy, you lifesaver! Will you ferry this little gobstopper somewhere safe and as far from here as you can? He might want some food, too."

"Sure thingummy," said Tippy, sweeping the drooling, apple-cheeked toddler into her arms. "Who's a good boy now, Artie-poo? Who wants a good warm bun from the oven? Come on now with your very best and only Tippy."

Artie looked intrigued. "Ceepee?"

"*Tee*pee," Tippy corrected. "Can you say that? Tee. Pee. That's me!"

And they warbled off across the square.

With that taken care of, Juniper turned her attention back to the field. Oona and Sussi had joined Alta in tying up the guards, while Filbert, Toby, and Roddy were dragging the rest of the fallen soldiers up from the crowd onto the stage. They began lining up the sleeping soldiers in neat rows like so much bundled cordwood.

The rest of Team Goshawk—Erick, Root, and Leena, as well as Egg—converged on Juniper as they awaited their next instructions. Juniper beckoned them toward the front of the fallen crowd, and headed that way herself.

Up on the stage, the Mantis had stopped calling for guards *and* had apparently decided to ignore Cyril altogether. She turned her full attention on Juniper, her gaze raking like claws. "Who *are* you?" she hissed. "I could almost swear that I've—"

Juniper didn't give her the chance to pursue this train of thought. Brushing aside Erick's grip on her arm, she vaulted three piled-up schoolboys and a portly merchant whose dozing frame held no fewer than five portable timepieces. In a bound, she was onstage—much like leaping onto the back of a horse, come to think of it.

The rush was the same, too: that is, if the leap was to bring you face-to-face with your archenemy and the tyrant who had overtaken your entire country and imprisoned your royal father.

Cyril shifted so his sword hovered just below Malvinia's breastbone. She clicked her tongue impatiently but stopped moving.

Juniper clambered to her feet and yanked at the pull-tie of her cloak. With one grand gesture, she threw it across the stage. She straightened her stance, jammed her hands onto her hips, and stared the Mantis down, glare for glare. The royal position felt unfamiliar around the rough-sewn trousers and knee-high boots she was packed into. Without her cloak, the wind blew fresh currents of air through her shortened curls and down her back.

Cyril lowered his sword and stepped back, letting his stepmother look full in Juniper's face.

"*You!*" Malvinia's eyes widened in recognition. "The little Torrence brat? But how . . ."

That was all Juniper needed. It had been an indulgence, that moment of big reveal. She'd have been better off going straight for action. But sometimes you just needed to pause long enough to give audience reaction its due. That accomplished, Juniper sprang to action. She strode across the stage and let her voice ring out loud: "Malvinia Lefarge, you are a traitor to the crown of Torr. I am hereby placing you in custody."

Malvinia curled her lips in a sneer. "You must be joking. The crown of Torr is *mine*. It's my due and my right. You and your puny band of playacting kiddies don't stand a chance."

Juniper had said all she needed to. Now she nodded at Cyril, and at Alta, who had used the lull to fetch her own sword, and now stood in a mirror pose to Cyril on Malvinia's other side. "Please restrain the impostor," said Juniper. "Gently, but double-check those knots. She's a slippery one."

"You'll regret this," Malvinia hissed. "Every single one of you. I'll make sure of it." She spat at Cyril. "And you most of all."

At this, Cyril looked thoughtful. Then, making sure that Alta had her sword fixed upon Malvinia, he leaned in closer.

"Stepmother," he said conversationally, "there's something you should know. I have been replacing each of my father's food trays for the past three days. As well as providing him with extra purifying and fortifying medicines, which I got for him myself from the Bazaar. You will be gratified to hear that this morning he regained consciousness at last. He's not fully lucid yet, but I expect that by tomorrow or the day after, he shall have some very interesting tales for us."

Malvinia's eyes widened, then narrowed to two hateful slits.

Cyril caught a round of rope that Roddy threw him and set to work tying her up. Beginning with a firm gag across her mouth.

Across the stage, the woodpiling of the guards continued. Erick had joined the group and was instructing the others in arranging them in groups of two: back to back, hands tied tightly to hands and feet to feet. It was a creative bit of knot-work, in which Erick seemed to take an almost artistic delight. Or maybe it was just the joy of enacting something from one of his beloved instructional volumes.

Finally the guards were taken care of, and the Mantis was

tightly bound and gagged and seated back on her makeshift throne. Her eyes, though, spoke of violence to come.

"You brought this on yourself," Juniper said to her. "My father will pass judgment on you just as soon as we've freed him. Which is what we're on the way to do next. Surely you can see that you've lost this battle."

The Mantis jerked her head forward into a violent head butt, which Juniper barely dodged. "Tsk, tsk," said Juniper, and leaned in to check the woman's waistband. A moment later, her fingers closed around a heavy key chain. "I've got it!" she called.

Malvinia growled low in her throat. Her shoulders shook with rage.

Juniper spun around and placed the key ring in Alta's hand. "Can I leave this part in your capable hands? Take Root and Filbert with you. We need reinforcements, and we need them now—I have no idea how long it will take for other palace guards to get wind of what's happening and come against us. We need to get control of the palace in the next quarter hour or the whole thing is lost."

"Understood," said Alta, but she hesitated.

"What?"

"You know it's going to be near impossible to get into that dungeon, don't you? It's guarded head to tail."

"I know, but we need it done," said Juniper simply.

Alta nodded and signaled to Root and Filbert. The three left without a backward glance.

And right then was when Juniper heard the loud sound of a horn. The low rumble of castle gates being drawn open. The *clackety-clack-thump* of horses' hooves and marching feet stamping along a packed gravel road.

"What on earth?" she said, spinning in place. Then Egg was at her side, and Juniper realized she hadn't been on the stage while they'd been dispatching the Mantis and her guards. Now Egg's breath came in quick bursts, and two spots of red burned in her cheeks.

"The Monsians," she scribbled in a rush. "They have arrived."

Seeing this, Juniper froze. It was not even sunset—how on earth had the Monsian delegation covered so much ground so fast? They weren't supposed to be here for hours yet! By to-morrow morning—or a few good hours from now, even—the Queen's Basin team would have broken all the soldiers out of the dungeons; they'd have retaken the castle; they'd have freed King Regis.

The battle would have been over and the gate guards under their control, if only the stupid Monsians could have come when they were supposed to.

Instead, what would the Monsians find when they came around that bend in just a few minutes? A group of kids playing keep-away, that was what. A tied-up ruler (impostor though she might be) and a stack of log-piled guards.

Juniper and her friends wouldn't last a hot minute.

What she *really* needed was to know whether Paul had gotten through safely, whether even now there was a counterforce of Anju heading in their direction. Now that she thought about it, the timing instructions she'd given Paul weren't nearly specific enough. If there was just one thing Juniper could have asked for in life, it would have been for things to happen right when they were meant to. A schedule, for crying out loud! Was it too much to ask that all future battles submitted a specific schedule to her first for approval?

"How many men are with them?" she asked Egg.

Egg flashed her hands out, fingers splayed, five times.

"Fifty men? Soldiers?" Juniper asked.

Egg nodded.

"Are they armed?"

Egg nodded.

Juniper felt her knees weaken. To think that a fighting band of fifty armed Monsians could just waltz in the front gates of Torr Castle! With a dull rush, Juniper realized her error in not sending all her forces to secure and close the front gates. Yet what would that have accomplished, other than alerting the guards stationed there to come to Malvinia's rescue? Well, there was nothing to do now but roll with whatever was coming their way. "Let's get things ready here, then," she said grimly.

From her spot on her throne, the trussed-up wannabe queen of Torr skewered them with her gaze. Despite her bonds, the Mantis managed to remain both haughty and condescending, as though she were just waiting for this playact to be over so the naughty rebel children could be put to bed without their supper.

Well. They would see about that!

Juniper and the crew claimed the stage as their standing ground. With Alta, Filbert, and Root gone, as well as Paul, they were low on fighting power, but what the rest of them might lack in brawn, they made up for in raw fierceness.

"Anyway, you've got me—what else do you need?" said Cyril, flashing a cheesy grin.

Juniper rolled her eyes at him.

"All them soldiering lessons Alta gave us in the Basin are gonna come in handy now, aren't they?" said Leena with tremulous glee.

The others didn't seem quite as excited, but at least nobody was turning to run from the Monsians, whose clanking armor and clattering wheels now rang through the courtyard like a thunderstorm looming to break.

Sussi passed around the Bobcats' balancing poles, the longer of which Roddy cracked neatly in half to arm as many of them as he could. Egg pulled out her bow and held it at the ready. She and Cyril were the only ones with true weapons but, honestly, Juniper wasn't kidding herself. If it came to an actual fight, they had lost already. Raw fierceness aside, the only chance they had was making this into a battle of wills and wiles.

And so they stood their ground. Nine kids against an invading army. A hand upraised against the enemy flood, as though by sheer force of will alone, they might save Torr.

Who else was there to do it?

26

THE NEXT TEN MINUTES OR SO PASSED IN TENSE silence, as the clatter of the approaching army mounted ever louder in their ears. Juniper stood at the front center of the stage, trying to look tall and stern and regal. In truth, she knew that she looked short and scrubby, about as *un*royal as humanly possible in her chopped-off hair and sweat-stained britches.

But attitude? That she could put out in wagonloads.

Cyril stood directly in front of his captive stepmother, sword drawn as though daring anyone to approach. Leena and Roddy stood guard over the gaggle of guardsmen, some of whom had started to show signs of awakening—for all the good it would do them when they did. Egg had disappeared again, bow and arrows and all. Erick, Oona, and Sussi were circulating among the fallen crowds. Here and there, a head popped up and a voice croaked out a loud expression of alarm. To each of these confused wakers, one of them would run up with a quick explanation of what had happened and instructions to stay quiet and move to the edges of the square.

Within the next few minutes, a good portion of the fish-flopped masses was gradually replaced by attentive huddles of seated bodies. Erick and the girls did their job well: not a person ran or screamed or even showed visible fear. All eyes stayed fixed, wide and wondering and alert, every one watching the stage and the winding road that led in from the gates.

Then a tap on her shoulder drew Juniper's attention. Egg had reappeared, showing her armband.

"'Alta is stuck,'" Juniper read. "Wait, what do you mean?"

Egg shook her head, wrote more: "Not captured. Too many guards at dungeon. They can't get in. Need a distraction."

Draw the guards out from the dungeon? A grand idea, sure. But that would just plop them out of the pancake dish and into the syrup. Juniper and her crew were no better equipped to deal with attacking soldiers than was Alta. Arguably less so. In any case, Juniper could think of no way to do so, and she said as much.

Egg nodded, then patted Juniper's shoulder. She waved her hand at Juniper in a way that very clearly said, *Have you peeked into a looking glass lately?!* If Juniper couldn't look like a queen, or even a princess, ideally she should not look like a street urchin.

It was a valid point.

"Juniper!" came Sussi's shriek from down among the crowds. "They're here—this is it!"

Juniper spun around. Sussi was right: They were out of time.

. . . Or were they?

Juniper squinted up the road. The bannermen were just edging around the corner. "Hold that thought," she said. She hopped off the back of the stage and ran to the fountain. Leaning over, she ducked her head straight in. The cool water shocked and refreshed her. Then she slid her bone-handled comb from her sleeve and gave herself a stiff grooming. Patting her face dry, she smoothed her rumpled outfit. It wasn't much, but it would do.

Refreshed and reenergized with a spritz of princess power, Juniper leaped back to her place at the front of the stage.

Yes. *Now* they were truly out of time.

The Monsian contingent had arrived.

Now at full alertness, Juniper strode to the front of the stage. A quick glance showed her that Egg had disappeared again, no doubt gone back to assist Alta's team. How *did* that girl manage to move so fast and unobtrusively? Spy power, indeed. Cyril took a step back, shifting in tighter alongside his stepmother. Erick, Oona, and Sussi had finished their crowd wrangling and clambered back onto the stage. They stood to either side of Juniper. On the ground, a few newly woken Torreans started shifting in place, standing and moving around. *No!* Juniper thought. *Please don't bolt now.* What if they all started to run? Would the Monsians chase them?

But then she looked—*really* looked. A woman was striding with purpose across the crowds, and her face was suddenly familiar. It was the farmwife to whom they had given the coins. She looked straight at Juniper, gave a crisp nod, then turned to stand boldly on the ground before the stage. She held a long skinny loaf of bread in front of her like a weapon. Without a word, a man came to stand next to her, hefting a hamhock over one shoulder. Another joined them bearing a lumpy pewter jug. They kept coming one by one, each raising weapons of food or utensils or branches or nothing at all, forming a living wall between the stage and the encroaching Monsian army.

Juniper thought her heart would burst with pride and joy.

But now the Monsians filled her line of sight, and her mind had room for nothing else but their approach. Three enormous stallions led the way: Those on either side were black as night and mounted by burly bearded men in chain mail. Just behind walked two soldiers, each bearing a tall banner emblazoned with the scarlet wolf of Monsia. In the center rode a third horseman, and this was the one who drew the eye. Unlike the others, this rider was clean-shaven, tall, and spindle-thin so that even mounted, helmetless with his long hair blowing to the side in the evening gusts, his look was an eerie echo of his country's banners.

His eyes scanned the platform, taking in Juniper's bold stance, the others in position near and beside her, the scattered audience (including the fierce makeshift defenders), and the bundle of bound guards.

"Well, well, well," the newcomer said in a curt, gravelly drawl, bringing his party to a halt. "I'm not interrupting, am I? Perhaps we should step back out, give you a half hour to, er, resolve things among yourselves?"

In a bound, Juniper leaped from the stage and strode toward the new arrivals. Roddy and Toby scurried to follow beside her (they had each swiped one of the captive guards' swords, which reassured Juniper somewhat). Oona tagged at their heels. Cyril, Erick, and Sussi held their spots onstage. The crowds of Torreans shifted to make a path for her as she strode toward the Monsian intruders.

Ten or fifteen paces from the lead horse's muzzle, with the crowds a good ways back, Juniper stopped. She held out her arms to stop Roddy, Toby, and Oona, too, shifting them slightly behind her. "You may approach!" she called loudly.

Her heart hammered in her chest, but she kept her face as smooth as marble. By the goshawk, she was a princess and she was a *queen*! Drippy and disheveled, perhaps, but right now, she was all Torr had. She would not cower.

She *would* be enough.

The spindly man chuckled. "Oh, may I?" With a sort of shrug, he oozed off his horse, shook himself as though popping his limbs into shape, then stood tall.

Very, *very* tall. Juniper suddenly found herself squinting into the late-day sun. The dirt-blasted Monsian was nearly twice her height!

Still. Juniper ignored him and looked from side to side, refusing to be rushed. But her mind ran fast and furious. What information did she have? She skipped her gaze to the procession. Behind the five horses was a gilt carriage, clearly meant for the unnamed ruler who stood before her, when he tired of riding. A group of foot soldiers followed, all settling back into inattention. Behind them were several large sturdy wagons, one with iron-barred windows, and another glinting with wicked-looking iron contraptions.

Egg's assessment had been right: These Monsians were armed

to the teeth. They did not appear to have come to mount an immediate attack—they were clearly allies of what they'd thought was Torr's new ruler—but this was a suspiciously large weaponry for a talk among friends.

Juniper didn't like it one bit.

Taking a deep breath, tilting her head so far back her neck ached—but oh, she *would* meet him eye to eye!—Juniper blew her words out with the force of a trumpet. "Delegates of Monsia, you are trespassing upon the sovereign land of Torr. You come here with your banners furled and your swords visible. Who are you, and what is your purpose here today? For I guarantee you that things have changed since you last walked this ground some weeks ago. The chief difference is this: You are no longer welcome."

27

THE STICKLIKE MAN LISTENED TO JUNIPER IN silence. Then he bobbed his chin toward the stage. "Is that Malvinia Lefarge I see up there? You've taken her captive? You and your . . . little friends?"

Juniper bristled. "I neglected to introduce myself, and my rough outfit may have led you astray. I am Crown Princess Juniper Torrence. Our King Regis was betrayed and usurped from his rightful throne. My army is retaking the castle as we speak, and will soon have set him free." She paused. She hated to concede any uncertainty or weakness, but she had to know. "And you are . . . ?"

"I thought you would never ask." The man smiled ingratiatingly. "I am Garr, Scion of Monsia. Our country has lately come to an . . . agreement with Torr."

"I'm sure you did," Juniper spat. "And you can see what I think of your *agreement*."

At this, the Scion burst out in a loud, long laugh. It didn't sound evil or even particularly harsh. It mostly sounded baffled, like he genuinely had no idea what was going on or how the world had suddenly gone so strange. "Child," he said at last, while Juniper's neck steamed inside the stupid collar of her stupid boys' vest and shirt. "Child, *what* are you doing? You need to step aside and let the grown-ups figure out these thorny issues of state. All right? We'll just dust all this under the carpet and never speak of it again. Now, do be good and let me talk with Malvinia Lefarge."

Behind Juniper, the crowds shifted uneasily. How, how, *how* could she get this man to take her seriously? Juniper was used to being overlooked, viewed as nothing more than a pretty princess, a decorative item to be swirled in lace and paraded around the palace. She'd never minded much before. Then again, she'd never before had so much at stake. And, if she was honest, the long weeks she'd spent ruling Queen's Basin, and competing alongside the Anju, had done a lot to reshape her outlook on life.

She saw herself differently now. She knew her own worth.

And she was hanged if she would ever let herself be underestimated again.

"Malvinia Lefarge is a traitor to Torr. She has been dealt with and will be judged in accordance with our laws." With pleasure, Juniper heard the cold steel in her voice. She thrust a steady hand up toward the Glassroom, where a figure could easily be seen, standing with both hands on the glass, looking down at the proceedings. "Do you see what has become of my father, King Regis? He has been imprisoned by this villain. But I assure you that his liberation is imminent."

A loud crash came from inside the castle. With it, fainter but growing in volume, the clank of steel on steel and the mounting bellow of voices. Alta had found her opening! The Scion evidently heard it, too. He tilted his head in puzzlement.

Juniper's heartbeat quickened. "As you can hear for yourself, my people are freeing the captive Torrean army and retaking the castle. The traitors will be behind bars shortly, and then we shall see justice served." She could only hope this was the case. But the sound of battle was heartening; the three insurgents hadn't just been bumped off. Fighting meant that there were enough people free and alive to fight. And as Juniper herself had learned, the newly freed had an extra vigor for battle that was all their own. Desperation is a fiery thing, driving people to heights they'd otherwise think impossible.

Now there was just one last thing needed to bring the whole thing together. Where, oh, where were the Anju? Paul had been gone for several days—how long could that journey take? She knew the Anju were fast runners. Surely they would be here soon. *Surely.*

Behind her, the Scion made an impatient growl at the back of his throat. His forces might not have their weapons at the ready, but any time he set his mind to it, they could overpower Juniper's supporters in mere minutes.

No, they couldn't wait any longer. Juniper would simply have to leap, and hope that solid ground would form itself beneath her feet.

This was becoming a bit of a habit lately.

In front of her, the Scion's face had pinched shut. His bushy brows were drawn together in one unhappy caterpillar line. "I'm sure you are——" he began.

Juniper leaped. "That's not all. In the past weeks, I myself, Crown Princess Juniper of Torr, Ruler of the Dominion of Queen's Basin and temporary Regent of Torr (until we free my father), have made contact with the reclusive Anju people."

There was an audible intake of breath—from the Scion, but also from his near guards, and those in her supporting crowd who were close enough to hear the exchange.

"That's right," said Juniper, warming to her delivery. "Everything you have heard about these awe-inspiring people is true. For centuries they have kept to themselves, but no longer. For the Anju have now forged an alliance with Torr. The people of the Hourglass Mountains have pledged their help to our nation when we need it and when we should call on them for assistance."

The Scion barked out a churlish laugh. "Surely you don't expect me to believe——"

"The Anju kingdom is formed of dozens of tribes situated all through the Hourglass Mountains. Do you really want to pit yourself against an entire network of peoples?" Juniper raised her voice to a shout.

And it was just then, at this most delicious and pertinent of moments—though, in Juniper's opinion, having stalled this speech as long as she could, the moment would have been welcome a good quarter of an hour ago, at least—that a great bluster of wind whipped through the square.

Someone in the crowd thrust a finger toward the sky and

211

screamed. Others whipped their cloaks around their heads. Still more dropped flat on the ground. The Scion's head craned back, his eyes bulging, tracking the great copper monstrosity that now circled in the sky above the Small Gardens. For Juniper and her friends, the creature was a familiar, even welcome sight. But she knew what this looked like to the rest of the onlookers: a giant draco, airborne, long of teeth and terrible of claw, a creature never before seen in living memory.

From the great fiery draco's mouth came a burst of white-blue flame, which hit the fountain squarely in its basin, boiling the water to a cloud of scalding steam. On the draco's back, a figure could clearly be seen, riding with legs astride and lifting arms overhead in a fierce shout.

The Anju had arrived.

28

EVEN BEING FAMILIARLY ACQUAINTED WITH
the fiery draco known as Floris—more than acquainted; Juniper
had *ridden* that glorious beast herself on one memorable afternoon—
even so, the display of firepower was impressive. Very few of those
watching knew how tame and friendly the draco actually was.
(Juniper knew it was no accident that the blast of flame had gone
into the pool of water.) As the enormous wings beat closer, Juniper
saw that riding on Floris's back was Zetta, her former rival and now
the ruler of the Anju people. To Juniper's astonishment, a second
head peered from behind Zetta's back. This showed a fairly green
face, and now that Juniper looked, she could see arms like iron
bands clamped to Zetta's waist.

It looked like Paul was getting the ride of his life!

Juniper swallowed a grin and turned back to the quavering
Scion. It was time to raise her showmanship to its highest level.
Floris had upped the game.

"NOW!" Juniper bellowed, directing her words not just to

213

the Scion, but to the entire Monsian army, to the trussed-up Mantis and her captive guards, even to the crowds of Torrean on-lookers on the edges of the gardens—so that *all* would hear and know. "Representatives of the kingdom of Monsia, *now* do you see and believe?! Do you really want to align yourself not only against Torr, but against the combined forces of the greatest mass of people in the Lower Continent? And their most deadly firepower?"

The Scion cleared his throat. He swallowed convulsively, but still seemed to be having trouble forming words. Finally he sput-tered, "We need not be too hasty, after all. Monsia is a neutral country. We have kept out of such skirmishes—"

"You have done no such thing!" Juniper thundered. "Your help made this invasion possible. Your armies battered our gates and enacted this takeover. And now *you* enter our land with your horse-men and your foot soldiers and your wagons heavy with arms."

A patter of hoofbeats rippled through the line of Monsians as a page on a wiry pony jogged up to the front. He was panting loudly, and Juniper could just make out his words as he addressed the Scion. "Sire, there is a whole column of warriors making their way down the Highway—a hundred, maybe more. They have a strange sort of weaponry and look fierce as can be. They are moving at a steady run and will be at the gates in under a day. I came to tell you right away."

Juniper nodded in satisfaction. Zetta had delivered on her promise: The rest of the Anju were on the move.

The Scion of Monsia looked again at the circling Floris. Then he studied Juniper as though seeing her for the first time. "Your

Highness Princess Juniper," he said at last. "Will you walk with me? I believe we have much to discuss, you and I."

Juniper looked him squarely in the face. What she *really* wanted to do right now was drop everything and go and free her father. But she knew better than to leave the Scion alone; their agreement was not quite so assured yet that she felt comfortable turning her back on it. Plus, she hadn't gotten the all clear from Alta; the palace wasn't fully freed yet.

"Very well," she said. She narrowed her eyes at the Scion. "I will make time for a short dialogue. But first you shall remove all weapons from your person. And your entire army will leave the grounds of Torr Castle *immediately*!"

As they walked the ornamental maze, through the sculpted hedgerows and around twisting corners, the Scion of Monsia assured Juniper over and over that he'd had no ill intentions in reentering Torr—that he had done so only on the invitation of Malvinia, then-ruler that he assumed she was. The pileup of weaponry in those wagons made Juniper doubt this, but she let him carry on with his story. The Scion went on to tell the same backstory that their group had pieced together days before—along with a few missing pieces of his own. He confirmed that Malvinia Lefarge had her distant roots in Monsian nobility, though her family had married into Torrean society many generations back, before the divide between the two nations. Since discovering her many-times-great-grandmother's unused Golden Bequest twelve years before, Malvinia had begun scheming for the throne of Torr.

Rupert Lefarge had been a mere stepping-stone in that plan right from the start—a morose widower with a young son, but with good blood and connections, and well placed within the palace. Marrying him had been the perfect key to advancing her plan.

"But these Golden Bequests," Juniper said, "they can't be very common, can they?"

"It is, essentially, one limitless gift from the throne of Monsia," the Scion said. "The bearer may ask for anything within the power of Monsia to give. Thus, 'not common' is an understatement. A Golden Bequest has been issued perhaps a half dozen times over our entire history."

Juniper whistled low. "That's something!"

"Indeed. It is more a thing of legend than of fact." He smiled thinly. "Much like your winged monster out there."

Juniper was not letting her subject go yet. "So the Mant—that is, Malvinia—cashed in her Golden Bequest, and she asked for the throne of Torr?"

"In a manner of speaking. Clearly, the throne of Torr was not in my power to give. But what she demanded was the fighting force to bring invasion to these walls. And you must know that she and Lefarge enacted their own betrayal, causing the gates to be opened to allow our entry. We ourselves had no wish to set soldiers on Torrean soil, believe me."

"So this one woman and her Bequest twisted your arm, that's what you're saying? *Forced* the Monsian crown into action against its will?"

The Scion shifted uncomfortably. "She did go, er, public with her Bequest. She spread the word far and wide. The crown had no choice but to act, or risk losing all face and credibility among the people."

"You're saying you had no excuse but to attack Torr."

"Monsia did not attack Torr! Far from it. We would never dream of provoking our near neighbors in this fashion." He looked so piously righteous that Juniper almost laughed.

"You are really saying that you see a difference between going to beat somebody up because you want their dinner, and sneaking into their house with a big stick to stand there and force them to give their dinner to somebody else?" Juniper thought that was a pretty nifty analogy, but the Scion was unmoved.

"I do not expect you to understand, young as you are, but when it comes to a Golden Bequest, this monarch's hands are truly tied. Nevertheless, our agreement ended the moment Malvinia Lefarge claimed the throne. I give you my word, Princess Juniper: Monsia bears no ill will against Torr. It is true that our countries have drifted apart in recent generations. Yet we wish no enmity with you. And we would never willingly raise arms against your people."

"You did, though," Juniper said pointedly.

"If you cannot see that the Monsian throne was honor-bound to do so, even to our own hurt, then you are less astute than I thought," the Scion retorted. "Be that as it may, even without the introduction of the Anju into the field, as I said: Monsia bears no grudge against Torr. We came here on the express invitation of Malvinia Lefarge. You can see that I brought no army—this guard was for basic protection only."

Juniper didn't believe him for a second. She could, however, take his current position at face value. His odious soldiers were now safely outside the walls, and before the sun set would be scooting back to their country with their collective tail between their collective legs. The Mantis had been subdued. The full Anju army was on the way. The loyal palace guard had been freed (or Juniper hoped they had; the noise of battle had grown noticeably quieter).

And now, at long last, they would be able to free her father.

"My father will wish to speak with you, I am certain," she said at last. She thought a moment, then gave a crisp nod. "Scion Garr of Monsia, I accept your assurances of a renewed peace between us. So long as the entirety of your forces remains outside of the gates, I shall allow you—and only you—to enter the palace and make yourself comfortable while awaiting my father's pleasure."

"Assuming the palace *has* been retaken," said the Scion, with a glint in his eye.

Juniper bristled. "Yes," she snapped. "And I'd best be off to see to that, hadn't I?"

When Juniper emerged from the maze, she saw that Floris had landed directly in front of the fountain. Unsurprisingly, there was a large clear space around him, though the number of gawking townspeople had tripled since Juniper had left. Word of the novelty was spreading.

"Juniper! There you are," said Alta, running up. Her hair was disheveled, and she had a streak of mud across her nose, but her eyes were bright and blazing.

"How did things go back in the palace?" Juniper asked.

"Smashingly," said Alta. "It took us some time to bypass the guards, but finally Root caused a distraction and we got in. Dropped a bag of hazelnuts—wouldn't you know it? The darn things went everywhere, people were sliding all over the place, with no idea how or why. Those blasted things blend right in to the stone, so you can't see them for a wink till they're underfoot and then it's nose in the air, and splat. Once we got the first few cells open, we had enough forces to retake the whole palace in record time. The traitors gave themselves up almost immediately—nobody wanted to be on the wrong side if the king was back in power."

"And my father?"

"He's still up in the Glassroom. We've just removed the guards down below, and I thought you might want to—be the one to, you know."

"I sure do," said Juniper. She looked across the grounds to where the tall greenhouse-turned-prison glowed gently in the waning light. Climbing those stairs would take a long time, and getting back down even longer. Her father had to be weak from his captivity. Juniper's eyes shifted. She caught the eye of Zetta, who stood guard over her friend and prize.

Floris?

Zetta nodded ever so slightly.

Floris.

29

JUNIPER'S SECOND FLIGHT ON FLORIS LACKED the breathless unexpectedness of the first, but was no less thrilling for that. Zetta climbed on first and lowered a hand to pull Juniper up after. Floris's broad back had plenty of space, so Juniper called Erick up at the last moment.

Her friend's eyes widened. "Me?" he asked, with the clear expression of one who is so used to experiencing his adventures within the pages of a book that he can't quite reconcile meeting one in real life.

"You," Juniper confirmed. "Come on! My father is waiting."

Then they were on, the great beast spread his wings, and off they gusted on the back of the winds. In the buffeting airstream, Juniper thought the small Glassroom—barely the size of Floris himself—looked impossibly precarious, like the head of a tall sunflower overlooking the castle grounds.

"How—are we going—to get—from here *in there*?" Erick said in her ear. His hands were iron bands around her waist, and she could feel his shoulders quivering behind her. She had been no better on her first ride and, truthfully, was just barely keeping herself together on this one. Still, she squeezed his hand as reassuringly as she could.

"Have no fear," Zetta yelled from the front. "We've got a trick or two, Floris and I."

As they approached the Glassroom, Juniper's heartbeat quickened. Through the crystal walls, a shape could be clearly seen—a comfortingly stout body, a head topped with gray, a face all lines and creases, eyes now wide with shock and concern.

"PAPA!" Juniper screamed. And then he looked past the mass of draco flesh and he saw her.

His face lit up.

Zetta scooted Floris up next to the little platform at the top of the climbing ladder. Juniper hopped off, with Erick behind her, while Zetta took off to circle Floris and prepare him for the return trip.

Juniper flung herself at the Glassroom door . . . and nearly bounced right back off. They kept it locked? When it was this high up and this well guarded? Juniper was well past the time for thinking clear thoughts. But she didn't have to, for Erick snagged a key from a peg on the outside of the landing and slid it into the lock.

The king had been watching all of this with raised eyebrows. When Erick pushed the door open, Juniper burst through it, and the next moment she was in her father's arms. They clung together, and she buried her face in his shoulder so he wouldn't see how the tears poured from her eyes. After so long, to hold him, to feel his comforting warmth! He was thinner than she remembered, but everything else about him was familiar and just right.

He was safe. All was well.

"Junebug, my darling girl! What the goshawk are you doing here?" her father said at last. Then he peered behind her out the glass. "And what in the name of everything is that *beast*?"

Juniper leaned back and brushed her eyes with her hand. "There's so much to tell you, Papa! But the important thing is that everything's under control now. Torr is safe. We've come to rescue you. There'll be treaties to ratify now with the Anju *and* with the Monsians. And a bunch of traitors to put on trial. You're needed."

Regis looked flummoxed. "What—how—" Then he smiled. "Ah, my Junie. You've been keeping busy in my absence, haven't you?"

Juniper grinned. "As always! And I didn't even need a schedule to do it." She tilted her chin toward the blue flower wreath. "I see you got my message, too. And I got yours."

"Nearly chipped a tooth on that meatloaf 'message,'" he quipped. He pulled the stone out and slid it into her hand. "But yes, I knew right away it had to be from you. Caused me more than a few sleepless nights, I'll tell you. I'd thought you were safe in the Basin!"

"I know you told us to stay there," said Juniper, squeezing the stone tightly and tucking it into her pocket. "But we had to come back. You see that, don't you? We couldn't let the bad guys win. We had to come back and try to help."

"Well, I can't argue with your results." Her father leaned back, holding her at arm's length. "You even look a little different. I can't quite put my finger on *what* the change is, but I could swear there's something . . ." He waved a hand at her vaguely.

Juniper laughed out loud. People she'd known for years couldn't recognize her through her disguise, and her absent-minded father couldn't figure out what had changed? "Never mind, Papa," she said. "I haven't changed in any way that matters. Not on the outside at least."

She grabbed him for another tight hug and wished she never had to let go. "Oh, the stories I have to tell! I can't wait to explain everything from start to finish. And there's ever so much still to do—all those historical treasures of Torr? They're still up in the mountains. We'll have to make a trip back to get them, wouldn't you say? And when we get there . . . Oh, I don't properly know where to begin catching you up!"

There was a tap on the window: Zetta, tossing a pebble to get their attention.

Juniper quirked her lips. "I guess now's not the time for it. Let's get you out of this cell, shall we?"

Right on cue, Floris pulled up outside the front glass. Erick opened the door. They stepped out into the whipping wind.

And so it was that King Regis made his debut ride on the back of the fiery draco, with his daughter close at hand and Zetta of the Anju as their guide. Erick graciously offered to make his own way down the long climbing staircase, not wanting to overtax Floris (and perhaps having also had enough nonbookish excitement for one day).

The first command King Regis gave when he reached solid ground was to raise the Torrean flag back to its proper place, unfurling it from the highest rampart of the castle. The flag of Monsia was brought down at the same time, of course, which the palace guards did with great distaste. Even the Scion of Monsia looked embarrassed when the wilted flag was returned to his care.

Hostile takeovers could be so awkward!

From there, King Regis and the Scion of Monsia held a brief but cordial exchange—a historic moment, to be sure; the first time the two rulers of these archenemy nations had been in one room since time out of mind. Then everyone retired to their chambers for the night—the moon being already high in the sky and the midnight hour not far off. There would be plenty of time on the morrow, the king declared, to think about treaties and trials and the like.

Malvinia Lefarge was locked away in the dungeons, under strictest guard. It was whispered around that her greatest regret was not having held the coronation ceremony at the start of Summerfest, so that she could have felt what it was to wear a queen's crown, even for a day. Rupert Lefarge had regained full consciousness and was now under guard in his chambers, until he was restored to full health. Malvinia's double-cross notwithstanding, Lefarge was fully responsible for his own betrayal, and Juniper knew he would have to pay the price. Her heart ached for Cyril, but at least his own change of heart and role in winning back the kingdom had caused the king to issue him a full pardon.

Rogett Ceward and Jessamyn had made a clean getaway; an eyewitness had seen them legging it north on horseback as fast as they could go. *Let them,* Juniper thought, *and good riddance.* They hadn't done anything illegal, not really (unfortunately, being a backstabbing coward was not against the law), but she had a feeling it would be a long time before they showed their faces in these parts.

Egg was offered a permanent place at the palace, if she desired it. Torr could do with its own in-house spymaster, the king proclaimed. "And I could do with having such a loyal friend near to hand," Juniper said. Remembering the sign Jess had taught her back at the start of their adventure, she brought her flat hand to her mouth and then ducked it down and out. *Thank you.*

Egg's eyes opened wide, and she grinned. She hooked her two index fingers together and twisted them. "Friend," she said aloud.

Juniper copied the sign. "I've got a whole lot to learn," she said. "I hope you'll be around to teach me." As Egg swept her into a big hug, Juniper knew her friend wasn't going anywhere soon.

Meanwhile, the dungeons were absolutely packed with the traitorous palace staff and soldiers, who had been stripped of all titles and responsibilities.

"We'll go easy on them," the king confided to Juniper as they sat on the couch in his outer chambers (which had been promptly cleared of anything Mantis-related). Two days had passed since his release from the Glassroom, and Juniper thought her father looked nearly as good as new. "After all, they had a pretty dire choice, with families to care for and doubtless fearing for their lives. But a couple nights in the cells will give them time for reflection, and hopefully provoke greater loyalty if it comes to such a choice again."

Juniper shuddered. "May it never."

"Junie," her father said, turning to grab both his hands in hers, "I haven't properly thanked you. How did you do all this, my girl? You saved our whole country—do you know that?"

Juniper grinned. "Don't worry about that, Papa dear. Honestly? It was kind of fun. And I didn't do it alone. I had the best band of friends and country folks you could imagine. We're Queen's Basin, don't you know?"

King Regis laughed. "I do know. Best edict I ever made, that one. Queen's Basin is a country worth its salt, and I mean it." He squeezed her hand tight, then held it up for a closer examination. "Look what it's done to you, though!"

Juniper looked. These weren't the soft, manicured hands of the cossetted princess who'd set out from Torr at the beginning of the summer. These hands had hard calluses from lugging paving stones across the Basin, scratches from forging rough territory during the Anju Trials, even a bruise or two from her fall when Jess drugged her in the dungeons. Juniper would not have traded those marred, ruined hands for any others in the world. "Every scar tells a story," she said. "And every one of them was worth it."

"How well I know it," her father mused.

"You have your own history with the Basin, I know."

"That I do." He sighed deeply as, in the adjoining chamber, the court musicians launched into a haunting rendition of *Belle and the Moon*.

• • •

The remainder of the Anju arrived at dawn the next day. Zetta had preceded them, flying as she had on Floris (and none too soon, either; Juniper shuddered to think what could have come of her delay), but had flown back out to join them for their grand entrance.

When the gates swung open with the sun, there they all were: Zetta standing tall and proud as their new young leader; Mother Odessa wearing—oh!—wearing Juniper's old cloak, which she had left on her last visit; tall and obnoxious Kohr, still standing stiffly at guard; even their former fellow competitors Libba and Tania (the latter of whom was sending significant looks Cyril's way, Juniper noted with interest).

As the Anju entered the gates, Torr's official welcome party awaited them: King Regis in his full royal regalia, with Juniper at his side in her mother's white cloak. Various nobles were present, as well as the Scion of Monsia, and of course the enthusiastic Queen's Basin crowd.

As the gates clanged shut against their stone buttresses, there was a moment's pause, a moment that hung like an ocean between the two separate groups. The history between Torr and the Anju was deep and personal. For an instant, it almost looked like that distance might be too wide to bridge.

Then King Regis swallowed and took three strong steps into the space between them. "Zetta of the Anju," he said, "I welcome you officially, and your people. You are my guests in the palace and in Torr."

"It is my pleasure to accept your hospitality," said Zetta, inclining her head, "for myself and my people." She lifted a hand, and three muscled men stepped forward, each carrying a large bundle, which they set down in front of the king. One contained masses of twinkling sweetcrystal, another overflowed with lustrous chamoix pelts, and the third contained a tall stack of the heat-conducting stone that was so common in the Hourglass Mountains.

Zetta continued, "Please accept these gifts as tokens of our friendship. Our people are known for being reclusive, but we wish to change this. Let this meeting launch a new time of cooperation between the Anju and Torr. Certainly our particular distance has personal roots; we hope that all will see their way to a reconciliation."

Her gaze went to Odessa, who stood straight-backed at her side. The king turned to stare long into Odessa's wizened, lined face. Something indescribable passed between the two, and Juniper thought of all the history they shared—anger and betrayal and silence and death, but most of all, love for the same woman: the king's wife and Odessa's daughter. Juniper's mother.

Then King Regis held out his arms to Odessa. "Mother," he said.

Odessa stepped forward to meet him. She clasped both his forearms with her own. "It has been long enough," she said.

That broke the dam, and in another minute, the two groups became one and swept away all obstacles in their path as they swirled into the castle grounds. Juniper noticed that Cyril made a beeline for Tania; she smirked and stored that fact up for later taunting.

"Hey," said Zetta, coming up behind Juniper and thumping her on the shoulder.

"Hey, yourself," said Juniper, grinning. "Is that the uncouth way rulers greet each other up in the mountains?"

"It's the only way between blood sisters," said Zetta.

"Not a bad speech you gave back there."

"You're not the only one who can rile up a crowd," Zetta retorted. "I can't believe I'm saying this, but I've missed you, Juniper, daughter of Alaina."

"And I you," said Juniper. "Is Floris being taken care of?"

"They've cleared out one of the stables for him to bunk in—can you imagine that? He's like a pig in a wallow. I'll have a hard time taking him home, I warrant. He'll be putting on airs about roughing it in his musty cave from now on."

Juniper grinned. "Well, he deserves some pampering. I heard the Scion of Monsia wanted a personal visit."

"We categorically refused! Floris is not to be trusted around enemy invaders of any stripe."

"I fully agree," said Juniper. "Oh, do tell me you will stay with us for a good while."

"We can't be here long, I'm afraid. There is much to be done back home, and the snows come early in the Hourglass. Plus, I hear that a cowed set of Monsian soldiers will be heading back north any day now. I thought we might provide them with an escort. Keep an eye on the retreat, so to speak."

"Oh, I like that idea!" Juniper grinned wickedly. "I wonder if Floris might not put a little fire behind their wheels?"

"I have a feeling he could be persuaded."

"Well, then, we'd better get busy enjoying the time we have together. And I can think of no better way to bond than you helping me plan a party."

"A party?"

"The party to end all parties. Anyone who's anyone in the whole Lower Continent will be here—haven't you heard?" There should also, Juniper mused, be a feast. Food and a giant dance party. What could be better?

Tomorrow was the final day of Summerfest, after all.

30

IN THE WAY OF ALL THE BEST EPIC FEASTS, THE
festivities began in the morning and would stretch languorously
through the whole day. A lavish breakfast buffet was set out in the
dining room: quails' eggs fire-roasted in their shells; soft cheeses
whipped to fine peaks and served on wispy crackers; delicate rose
petal jelly and carmine berry cobbler. Juniper had lost no time
after the takeover in fully shedding her disguise—disposing of her
sweat-scuffed trousers and triple-washing the last of the dark
tincture out of her hair—and now she chose a flowing gown of
palest green with matching orchid petal slippers. There wasn't anything she could do about her shorn locks, but she found that she
quite liked the way they curled softly around her ears, especially
when paired with a jaunty mauve ribbon.

All in all, she was feeling decidedly princess-like this morning.
She pushed with purpose through the swinging doors into the
bustling morning room, where the strangest assortment of guests
milled awkwardly around one another. The Scion of Monsia was

there, bulky and brusque in his ornate chain mail, which he had apparently chosen to wear since he was denied a personal guard. Zetta was there, along with Kohr and Mother Odessa, and several other prominent Anju, all wearing their lightest furs but still visibly sweating in the warm lowland weather. The Queen's Basin crew was there, and inexplicably Team Bobcat wore their balancing outfits, colorful feathers and all. The sleeping potion had been washed away and the garments were spotless, so this was evidently a deliberate choice. Juniper couldn't figure out what they were up to.

Alta came up (dressed in her own nonbalancing clothes) and grinned at Juniper's discomfiture. "They want to take their show on the road," she confided. "They liked performing that much. They figure if they stay in costume, someone might invite them to a far-flung city as guests."

Juniper laughed out loud. "And you?" she asked. "Back to your britches, I see."

Alta grinned. "I finally got my sword and scabbard. You think I'm going to give it up for a balancing mat? Not likely. I'm your royal guard, be you queen or princess or anything in between. I'm not leaving your side."

"Nor I!" came a shrill voice, and a pair of arms wrapped around Juniper's waist. "I'm your lady's maid for life, Your Very Juniperness."

"Tippy!" Juniper exclaimed. "I never thanked you for taking little Artie to safety. You saved the day."

Then she saw who was behind Tippy: the tall, awkward figure

of Tippy's older sister, Elly. To Juniper's surprise, Elly was now sporting enormous, bold-looking spectacles *and* a grin stretching from ear to ear.

"Your Highness Princess Juniper," said Elly, sinking into a curtsey. "I have so much to thank you for! You kept my rapscallion sister safe and brought her back to me even better than before, it would seem."

"You might almost say that *I* brought Princess Juniper," said Tippy, but Elly wasn't finished.

"It makes what I have to say all the harder—oh, you remember how clumsy I was when I worked for you?" Elly laughed. "It seems so long ago, but I was always falling over myself every moment of the day or night. Well, it happened that I was set in a dungeon cell with Mistress Talia, the chief librarian. She gave me her spare eyeglasses, and oh! How the world has opened up to me!"

Juniper digested this in silence. "They do, er, suit you," she tried.

"Not only that, but they have opened up a new profession. While confined within the cell, I began to study the mold formations along the dungeon walls. Do you know that in our cell space alone, I found more than eight separate types of mold?" Elly took a moment of silence to allow them to fully appreciate this. "All different! Can you imagine it?"

"Mold," said Juniper, not quite sure how to react.

"Forgive me, Your Highness, only I am that passionate about my new calling. Don't you see? I am to study molds! Such a field it is! I have already sent off my letter to the Academy, now that I am released, and my only regret is that I will no longer be able to serve you as a lady's maid and to demonstrate to you my newly acquired powers of vision."

"Oh," said Juniper. "Well. I'm sure we can arrange for something—someone—"

Right on cue, Tippy flashed her hands out in a dramatic pose. "Maid hands!" she said, beaming. Suddenly, Tippy froze. Her eyes went wide, and she cocked her head. "Could it—is that—might it really—" Then she threw up her hands and let out a piercing shriek. "FLEETER!"

Juniper turned. The door of the morning room stood ajar, and there, alone in a patch of sunlight, was Fleeter. The bedraggled cat was caked in mud. Half his fur stood on end, and the other half looked to have been chewed down to the pink skin of him. But his eyes were bright and his tail was straight, and when he saw—or heard—Tippy's call, he was across the room like a shot.

"Tippy, no! The thing must be infested!" Elly yelled. But it was no use. Tippy and Fleeter were together, and nothing would to pry them apart.

"Impressive," said Egg, then wrote on her armband, "Fleeter has never returned to a person before. Only a place."

Then Juniper remembered that on that last night, before Jess had taken Fleeter with her to the dungeons, Tippy had been feeding him some of that special mush that they used to mark where he should carry his messages. Tippy had only been giving him a snack; it looked like instead of bonding to a place, this time, Fleeter had bonded to Tippy's own self.

"Do you miss your father and sister a lot?" Juniper asked Egg. Amongst all of these joyous reunions, Egg's lack was glaringly obvious.

Egg bit her lip, then worked with her chalk for a moment. "I do. But I'm sure I will see them again. And meanwhile, I seem to have found a second family." The shy smile she gave Juniper warmed her right down to her toes.

As she and Egg moved off together toward the food table, Juniper looked around for the rest of Queen's Basin. There was Root, wedged in a corner next to a huge bowl of—what else?— hazelnuts. He was unwrapping a small parcel, while Oona looked on shyly. He pulled away the paper to reveal a fancy nutcracker, polished and gleaming. His face went scarlet with joy, and hers flushed to match. Then they both dug in to the nut bowl together.

At the opposite end of the room was Erick. He had two large volumes stuffed under one arm and held a third with a finger marking the place. But instead of reading, he was speaking animatedly to a tall man in a soldier's uniform—his father, the newly released and reinstated captain of the guard. At a key point in the story (their adventures in retaking the castle, no doubt), Erick had to set his books down and use both hands to illustrate some particularly active moment. It looked like father and son had found a way to connect at last.

The others were there too: Toby and Sussi sitting companionably together on an armchair; Leena studying her overstuffed food plate with a notepad in one hand as she appeared to conduct some taste-test or other; Filbert and Roddy horsing around on the edges of the room—were they actually arm-wrestling? Good grief! Paul was studiously ignoring his straight-backed, upright parents and their matched disapproving frowns. Well, not everybody could have a happy ending. She hoped that every one of her crew was in a better place than they'd been at the start of the summer, even in the smallest of ways.

But there was somebody missing.

And then there he was. Cyril burst into the room looking unusually disheveled. He spotted Juniper and straightened, but that did nothing for his creased clothing and bloodshot eyes.

"Cyril, what pit did you fall into?" Juniper asked, concerned. She reached up and picked something out of his hair. It was a very small sock.

"Um," Cyril said. "Artie had a rough night."

"Artie?" said Juniper. "You're watching your brother now?"

Cyril shrugged. "Who else is going to do it? I think the little tyke's had enough bad parenting for a while, don't you?"

Juniper shifted uncomfortably. "Does he have any idea about— you know, his mom?"

"He's way too young for that. And my father will be well again soon. Plus"—Cyril grinned—"she'll still get to have some part in his life. As it were, ah, remotely."

Juniper couldn't suppress a small giggle. Malvinia the Mantis, traitor and usurper, would stay locked safely in the castle's dungeons. But lest she suffer too much boredom, King Regis had decreed that she give much-needed daily help to the palace laundries. Now the personal touch she hadn't been willing to give her little boy could go into his messy play clothes, at least.

"Still," Juniper said, "it's got to be a lot of work for you in the meanwhile."

"Tosh!" Cyril stiffened his spine, and before Juniper's eyes, all the tiredness fell away. "He's a charmer right to the core. Kept me up till the wee hours telling stories. I'll get him to turn in earlier next time, just . . . " He smiled wide. "We were having a pretty decent time."

Juniper goggled. "Who even are you, and what have you done with my nemesis?"

Cyril grinned and punched her hard in the arm. "Always lurking when you least expect it. That's the way of nemeses."

"Is that so, *Ceepee?*" she said pointedly.

"Oh, no you don't! That name is entirely off-limits."

"Is it really?" Juniper mused. "Because I'm thinking of a new chant for my croquet game. It goes like this: 'Ceepee one, and two, and three! Ceepee loves to—' Ahh . . ." Juniper ducked Cyril's body block and ran for the gardens.

She'd had enough of being a queen for just this moment. Today, she was happy being just a princess, a cousin, and a friend.

The party began in the morning and built slowly throughout the day, but really came alive by high noon. By then, the kitchen staff had finished setting up the long row of tables that lined the entire walkway, from the fountain clear to the front gates.

Those gates were thrown open on the stroke of twelve o'clock. The enthusiastic—and exceedingly hungry—masses poured in and fell upon the tables, which had been heaped with all sorts of treats and delights.

When the food rush slowed at last, King Regis took the stage. He had a speech prepared, but before he could get a single word out, the cheering started. It started, and it did not stop, rising from the throats and hearts of the Torrean people, from youngest to oldest, all chanting and clapping and howling their approval.

Their king was back in his palace. Torr was safe.

He got their attention at last, when hoarse voices cracked and thirsty throats paused for another swig of punch. Then he cleared his throat again, and his booming voice echoed out over the entire courtyard. "My people," he said, "my beloved people." His voice broke, and he bowed his head.

The king never did finish his speech. But his sentiment could not have been clearer. He spent the rest of the afternoon mingling with the crowd, patting babies' heads and squeezing farmhands' shoulders, answering questions and giving reassurances. Juniper stayed right by his side, ready to spirit him away at any sign of weakness, but he stayed strong and unflagging. Midway through the afternoon, a familiar face pulled out of the crowd and came to stand before them. It was the farmwife to whom Juniper had given the coins. Her face was bright, and her gaze on Juniper was knowing.

"Your Majesty," the woman said, bowing low before the king,

then curtseying before Juniper, "Your Highness. I am glad the both of you are looking out for us in Torr. We couldn't ask for better."

The king turned an inquiring gaze on Juniper as the woman moved away, and Juniper smiled. "Someone we met on our adventures."

Her father's gaze turned thoughtful. "Speaking of adventures," he said, "wherever did you get that cloak? It looks somehow . . ."

She said, "It was Mother's," at the very same moment he said, "Familiar."

"Ah," he said.

"You recognize it."

He squared his shoulders. "I do. And there's a story there. I know . . ." He paused, seemed to reach inside himself for strength. "Your mother's passing was very hard on me. I know I didn't handle it in the best way—locking away all her belongings and never speaking of her. It's just, she meant so much to me."

"Don't, Papa. I understand—truly."

"No, I need to say this. I owe her more than to let her memory die away like this. So, yes, there is a story to this cloak. I don't have time to tell the whole of it now." He waved a hand at the crowds patiently awaiting their turn to speak to him. "But one of these days—maybe tomorrow, even—remind me, and I'll tell you a story. I'll tell you about how a young prince climbed a high mountain to live alone in the wild for a time; how instead of solitude he found the most beautiful girl he had ever known, and the kindest, and the bravest, and the wisest; how they fell in love, but secretly, for neither of their people would have understood." He smiled in remembrance. "That may have been the best summer of my life."

"When you were up in the Basin!" Juniper breathed. "You did build that platform up the Great Tree, didn't you?"

"You found my tree fort!" For a second, King Regis looked like a boy again, all impish flair. "We spent many hours together hidden in those branches, your mother and I. But the summer ended, and I had to go. After I got home, I had this cloak made specially for her: the finest weave and the newest, most precious fibers. I sent a messenger to bear it to her along with a declaration of my love and an invitation for her and her people to come to visit us in Torr."

Juniper's eyes opened wide. "That was what brought the party of delegates who came afterward, expecting to make a peace treaty. But instead . . ."

"Instead, Alaina chose to stay with me. She was sure that her mother—the chief of the Anju—would come around in time, that this union would bind our people together for good. But Odessa wouldn't do it. And by the time she changed her mind, it was too late."

It was a sad story, but hearing it filled an empty place in Juniper's heart. Just knowing made everything so much better.

She squeezed her father's hand. "I suppose you two have some catching up to do."

"I suppose we do. I've asked Odessa to stay awhile, and she's agreed. I thought you wouldn't mind."

Juniper felt a swell of joy inside her. "You thought right." And was the story truly sad, when followed through to its end? The torrent of pain had rushed through, for sure. But then it had gone, and in its place had grown up all of this new life she saw around her: her father, her people, her newly reconciled grandmother Odessa and all of the Anju, finally brought together just as her mother had always dreamed.

It can take time to grow a dream, Juniper thought. But every hard step along the way is worth it when the bloom springs to life at last.

Juniper had left Torr to follow her dream and had come to find that her dream had burst out from inside her very self, and followed her back. Maybe it took going away before you could properly find your true home. Now she saw it all—her father, her home, her people—in a completely new light. And they were beautiful. She could not have asked for a single thing more in the world.

And so she kissed her father on the cheek and ran off to join her new group of friends—not subjects, not a one of them, but true friends.

Up in the sky, a lone goshawk dipped low, circled, then flew off into the setting sun.

Acknowledgments

PRINCESS JUNIPER'S JOURNEY BEGAN OVER A decade ago, a snippet of story that wouldn't let me go. My pesky princess kept asking her question—"Might I have a very small country for my birthday?"—and I knew she wouldn't be satisfied until I pulled up a chair, dusted off my typing fingers, and gave her one.

It's now been two years since the release of *Princess Juniper of the Hourglass*, and Queen's Basin has gone on to thrive and prosper. The time has come at last to say good-bye. My greatest thanks go to you, my readers, who have come with me on this journey, and who are the ones who make it all worth doing.

Beyond this, I have to thank Jill Santopolo, editor extra-ordinaire, whose eyes were the first to light up, and who was the first to say YES to Juniper. Talia Benamy, who has been invaluable in ways great and small. Michael Green, Tara Shanahan, Venessa Carson, Alexis Watts, Carmela Iaria, and the whole Penguin team, for your support and guidance and encouragement along the way. My unflagging agent and friend, Erin Murphy, for absolutely everything. Erwin Madrid and Dave Stevenson, for your gorgeous artistry. Kirsten Cappy and Sarah Azibo, who have been instrumental in helping to spread the word and bringing in new readers.

My first readers and critique partners, as ever, are a huge part of this process, always there with essential input, advice, wisdom, encouragement, and a kick in the pants when I need it most. A huge thank-you to Julie Berry, Debbie Kovacs, Nancy Werlin, Julie Phillipps, Natalie Lorenzi, Kip Wilson, and Sarah Beth Durst.

I also want to extend a special thanks to my readers within the Deaf community, who generously read the manuscript and provided thoughtful and essential input to help me shape Egg's character and world: Marty Lapointe-Malchik, Will and Tracy Boland, Erika Guarino, Peggy Cryer, and Emily and Kathy Manfield. A million thanks to you all!

Last but not least, to Zack, Kimberly, and Lauren—thank you for your unflagging support, enthusiasm, and love. I love you always!